the map

of

us

Jules Preston

A division of HarperCollins*Publishers*
www.harpercollins.co.uk

Harper*Impulse* an imprint of
HarperCollins*Publishers*
The News Building
1 London Bridge Street
London SE1 9GF

www.harpercollins.co.uk

This paperback edition 2018

First published in Great Britain in ebook format
by HarperCollins*Publishers* 2018

A catalogue record for this book
is available from the British Library

ISBN: 9780008300975

Set in Birka by Palimpsest Book Production Ltd,
Falkirk, Stirlingshire

Printed and bound by CPI Group (UK) Ltd, Croydon, CR0 4YY

MIX
Paper from
responsible sources
FSC
www.fsc.org
FSC® C007454

Numbers are a poor measure of love.

Millicent Fenwick
Mathematician 1970-

the

map

of

us

Jules Preston was born in London, and has had lots of jobs. Some good. Some bad. The best was cutting up national newspapers with a huge pair of scissors. He now lives in Devon, surrounded by piles of paper held together with bulldog clips. One day they might get turned into books too. Hopefully.

🐦 @jules_preston_
f www.facebook.com/JulesPrestonAuthor

the beginning

Violet North could not walk far. She had a pleasing enough disposition and an inquiring mind, but she had lost the use of her legs as a child. Polio was the cause. She was now twenty-six years of age and not expected to marry. She had other complications from her childhood illness that meant she seldom left her home without the help of company. As she was not often seen outside, there were precious few who she could call upon for such assistance.

Her family had lately abandoned her in a house with several staircases and a large garden in the hope that she would fall and die as quickly and conveniently as possible. They had told her as much when they left. She had been a burden to them for long enough. Violet could not walk far, but she was twenty-six and had her own house with a large garden and decided to be as inconvenient as possible. She did a grand job.

Violet North had many interests beyond the confines of the front parlour in the summer and the study in the winter. She sent off for maps and globes of the world and invited those she knew to send her postcards from the places they had been. It did not matter where. Places that she would never see fascinated her. She read travelogues and the biographies of great explorers. For her, climbing the stairs to the third floor was an exhausting expedition, fraught with unknown dangers.

A photograph of the nearest railway station, no more than three miles away, was a particular delight to her. She knew she would never see it in person. Even if she could somehow surmount all the difficulties of getting there alone, how could she buy a ticket? She had no destination. Violet knew no one she could visit by train.

To occupy her inquiring mind and her passion for places that would forever be a mystery to her, she invented an explorer and a place for them to explore and wrote about their adventures on a Royal Quiet Deluxe typewriter that she borrowed from a neighbour. It was turquoise blue, and the 'e' often stuck.

The place that she invented looked very much like love.

I have seen it.

Violet North was my grandmother. And yes, that is where the journey to this started. Right there.

2 years ago

'Where do you think we went wrong?' Matt said.

'10.37am, April 22nd,' I said.

'Oh,' he said.

He put his glass down on the table and stared absently out of the window. A dog was barking at a paper bag somersaulting down the January street. I felt responsible. Not for the paper bag or the barking dog. I felt responsible because the absence that we both felt was my fault.

Sometimes people don't want simple answers. Most of the time, in fact. They say they do, but they don't. Not really. My soon-to-be ex-husband didn't. Not like that. Not right then. I could see him trying to compute the information. He was struggling. It was all too clinical. Too precise.

10.37am. The exact moment when our marriage fell apart. Or started to. Or finally shattered into a million unrecognisable pieces. He wanted something else. Something vague and meaningless.

'I don't know.'

Would have been good for starters.

'What do you think?'

Would have been a fairly safe follow-up.

He wanted to talk about it. I had just made sure that the conversation started without a heartbeat. I didn't do it on purpose.

'Oh,' he said again, as if that would resuscitate anything. It didn't.

I said nothing. That didn't help. What else could I say? I had already answered his question. And with a level of accuracy that I rarely manage to achieve in my day job.

I couldn't help myself. Me being me isn't always easy on those I love.

Loved.

Both. I guess.

It's complicated.

Read the report.

It's all in there.

Read it.

You'll see.

5 things about me

My mother always called me Matilda. Always. She was the only one that did. Everyone else calls me Tilly. It is who I am. More or less. I have an older brother called Jack and a sister that is older still called Katherine. No one has ever called her Kate or Katie. Never. They wouldn't dare. Katherine does not respond well to familiarity.

My father makes sand sculptures. He wears shorts and sandals and trails sand around wherever he goes. He drives old estate cars that are always French and don't like to start when it's damp. They are full of sand, too. And buckets and trowels and brushes and tarpaulins and tent pegs and half a dozen identical straw hats in different sizes to suit the prevailing wind conditions. When my father finds a slightly younger French estate car, he gives the old French estate car to me. Then I drive it until the wheels fall off. Literally. Or sand gets into something important and the engine seizes up. Whichever comes first, really.

I like numbers, but numbers have not always been my friend. Not always. We had a disagreement. Early on. We got over it.

It may have taken a reversing caravan to resolve the problem, but I cannot be sure. Numbers are beautiful and complex and do not always tell the truth even though you think they should. Numbers are not as straightforward as they seem. They have the capacity to lie and deceive and betray and confuse. That's why I work in statistics. I like numbers. We get on okay now. Most of the time anyway.

At the time, I was working for a company called Compass Applied Analytics. Their offices were on the first floor of a recently redeveloped building that once housed an industrial-scale launderette. They were called Super Efficient Laundry Services. You could still see where their name had been painted over on the wall outside. They had a logo, too. It was hard to make out, but I always thought that it looked like a pair of sprinting underpants.

My job was to compile sophisticated market research data for product evaluation and assessment. I specialised in low-fat snack bars for the health-conscious sector. I didn't eat them myself. I am health-conscious though. Not always. Sometimes. I prefer chocolate.

2 years ago (too)

'So, what do consumers think of the name?' The Marketing Executive from Bearing Foods asked.

'Loved the name,' I said.

'Uh-huh,' he said, writing something down.

'"Seedy-Pea-Nut-Slices" got a positive 86% approval rating from the focus group of average supermarket shoppers that we interviewed.'

'Pretty good figures,' Helen added, eager to be involved.

Helen doesn't usually attend my presentations on low-fat snack bars for the health-conscious sector. She's a strategist for new product development in the pre-packaged smoothies segment. She can't drink anything with pineapple in it though. It makes her tongue go numb.

Our head of department thought I might need a little moral support towards the end of the report. I disagreed, but I assumed that Helen being there was a sign that the company were taking no chances. Bearing Foods was one of our biggest clients.

'What about the packaging?'

'Loved the packaging, too. The packaging received a solid

75% approval. Potential customers thought it was fresh, bright and informative,' I said.

'Uh-huh,' he said, making another note.

'Without being too fresh, bright and informative to scare off an older demographic,' I added.

'That's a big thumbs up on the packaging,' Helen said. I nudged her with my elbow. She scowled at me.

'What about the ingredients?'

'Loved the ingredients. 79% approval on the ingredients. Peas, quinoa and seaweed were generally perceived as innovative, natural and nutritious. They loved the passive product claims, too. "Wholegrain." "Additive-free." "High in fibre." All had excellent penetration.'

'Great work on the ingredients,' Helen said, pumping the air with her fist.

'Uh-huh,' he said, thankfully not looking up from his notepad.

Pineapple, I thought.

I knew what was coming next.

'Visual appeal?'

Now this was where things got tricky.

'Not so good on the visual appeal of the product itself,' I said.

'Uh-huh,' he said, looking up this time. Helen crossed her arms and looked at me too.

'Only 29% of respondents were entirely positive about how the snack bar looked.'

'We had a few comments, too,' Helen said before I had a chance to stop her. '"Looks like squirrel poo," mostly,' she said.

'Uh-huh,' he said. The temperature in the conference room seemed to dip a few degrees. Maybe it was me. Maybe I was being overly sensitive. Helen took the awkward silence that followed as an opportunity to whisper in my ear.

'Sorry to hear that you and Matt have split up, Tilly.'

'Thanks, Helen,' I whispered back.

Pineapple.

'It must be difficult for you both,' she said.

'Yes. Thanks, Helen,' I said.

Pineapple.

'So, did your marriage last longer than the national average, or was it slightly less?' She sneered.

Suddenly it all made sense. This was payback for a comment I may have been overheard making about Helen being married and divorced twice in 64.726% of the national average. It was a statistics joke. We like that sort of thing around here. It was funny at the time. Helen waited patiently for a response.

Pineapple, I thought.

'Taste profile?' The Marketing Executive said.

I was glad that we were moving things on. The results for visual appeal were always disappointing with any granola-type snack bar. They all looked like rabbit food, or worse. 'Chewy' in the name didn't help. If it had 'Chewy' in the name, you could expect a further 6-8% drop in positive responses.

'Loved the taste,' I said. 'Significant approval ratings for the taste.'

'Uh-huh,' he said writing something down.

'Once they got over the fact that it looks like squirrel poo, of course,' Helen said.

'Uh-huh,' he said drawing a line through the thing that he had just written down.

Pineapple.

While I tried to murder Helen with the power of my eyes, he flicked through his notes dejectedly.

'So, what you're saying is that we have a fantastic product that could reshape the market in low-fat snack bars for the health-conscious sector if only it didn't look quite so much like squirrel excrement?'

'Essentially. Yes,' I said.

There was no getting around it.

'In a nutshell,' Helen said, trying not to grin.

'Uh-huh,' he said.

Pineapple, I thought.

'Seedy-Pea-Nut-Slices.' So many things to love. Just a few important things that weren't quite right.

A bit like Matt really.

2 years ago (still)

The bottle of 'sturdy' Rioja we had chosen tasted thin and vinegary. It wasn't our usual choice. It clung to the side of the glass in an odd way. I swilled mine around just to have something to do with my hands.

The table top was a slab of grey slate. It had a ring of wax where yesterday's candle had burnt down. I didn't pick at it. I wanted to though. I wondered how many other couples had sat where we were sitting now and had got together or broken up or talked about getting a dog or moving in together or celebrated or commiserated or decided to give it another go and had gone home hand in hand for the first time in months and made love and then separated for good. Maybe even while yesterday's candle was burning down to a stub. I could see where today's candle had been shoved into the candlestick holder on top of it and on top of other melted stubs for what looked like the passing of centuries.

'10.37*am*?' Matt said.

'Yes,' I said.

'Not 10.37*pm*?' He said.

'No,' I said.

'Oh.'

He looked more confused than ever. Somehow it bothered him that our marriage had come apart in the morning. Before lunchtime even. Not at night. Did it really make any difference? The end result was the same.

We were sitting in our favourite wine bar – that wasn't really 'ours' anymore – discussing who should take custody of the three-seater sofa from the living room. It had seen better days. So had we.

'10.37am,' Matt repeated absently. Like the title of a film that he had never seen, starring someone that he couldn't quite remember.

How could I be so exact? I had an affair. It started at 10.37am on April 22nd. It was a Thursday. I have a graph that explains why. Not why it was a Thursday – why it started at 10.37am. It's more of flow chart, actually. It's on Page 5 of the report. We'll get to that. Maybe later.

I didn't really want the sofa. But Matt did.

the marriage report

Okay. Maybe writing a report on our marriage with footnotes and a summary and a series of conclusions was another spectacularly bad idea. But that is what I did.

Matt just wanted to blame someone and feel betrayed and hang up on me all the time. I could see his point. But I wanted something more precise. I wanted to look at the distribution of fault and the relative impacts of known and random variables. Everything could be quantified and evaluated and interpreted using samples and controls and baselines – even the ups and downs of our relationship. I wanted to make sense of it all. I wanted a number. A simple diagram. Something that I could understand at a glance.

It was just another Bearing Foods presentation. It was no different. Not really. First, I had to identify my research aims. Then I had to gather evidence. When I had analysed all the available data, I could make informed statements and recommendations.

I chose to use a large lever arch file for my report. Something that would accommodate items of evidence that weren't all flat. I couldn't think of any items that might possibly fit that category, but I wanted to be prepared for the eventuality that one might crop up.

Matt and I had been married for three years. Our time together was like a low-fat snack bar for the health-conscious sector. A low-fat snack bar that had actually turned into something resembling squirrel poo. Now I was going to pick through the sticky ingredients with my fingers looking for answers. It was the least I could do.

clarity

I was in Trish Hudson's office. Trish is my boss. She's the head of the Statistical Analysis Department at Compass Applied Analytics. She is also quite short, so she wears irresponsibly high heels and has a blow-up cushion on her chair and wears a lot of vertical stripes because she thinks they make her look taller and thinner. They are only partially successful. She walks with a strange juddering totter because of her irresponsible shoes, and the thin vertical stripes make her look like a clump of dry grass swaying in a gale.

I get called to Trish's office quite a lot. I got called to her office the time that I was overheard making a comment about Helen being married and divorced twice in 64.726% of the national average. It was just a joke. But Trish doesn't think that statistics are a laughing matter. That's why she's the head of department. I suppose.

My trips to her office had been tapering off nicely. I was hoping this was only a blip in a long-term downward trend.

Trish looked like she had a wasp in her ear. That was fairly normal. She always looked like she had a wasp in her ear. When you got summoned to her office it was sometimes hard to tell if you were in trouble or not.

'Am I in trouble?' I asked.

'Yes,' she said.

That cleared that up then.

wasps

The cause of Trish's constant expression of irritated malevolence was the subject of much discussion and conjecture in the office.

Most speculated that it was the result of botched plastic surgery around the eyes in an attempt to make her look younger. The high heels and vertical stripes seemed to support the hypothesis. She already went to a great deal of effort to look taller and thinner.

Another, smaller contingent suggested that the blow-up cushion on her chair was not just to enable her to reach her phone but hinted at some chronic problem with her unmentionables. It was hard not to laugh at this one. For lots of reasons. None of them kind. I am a bad person. I admit it.

A third group thought that she did actually have a wasp jammed in her ear. Poor thing. The wasp, that is.

I'm not sure what I believed. It didn't matter now. I was fairly certain that the current look of squinty-eyed hostility had something to do with the Bearing Foods presentation earlier.

Blaming Helen would be futile. I knew that. Helen was the

only bridesmaid at Trish's lavish destination wedding last year. The venue was a remote island in the Indian Ocean that took 5 hours to get to by small boat. I wasn't invited. I'm glad I wasn't. It rained for nine days straight. I've seen the rainfall figures. They were the highest ever recorded. A little over 320% of the normal monthly average. It was impossible to get outside. In the end Trish was married in the main guest hut surrounded by overflowing buckets and the sound of palm trees being blown over.

Trish and Helen went to the same prestigious university too. I didn't. I went somewhere less prestigious that had an infamous nightlife.

On Fridays they sometimes shared a car to work. Neither had ever accepted a lift in mine. I could see their point. It used to belong to my father. It was full of sand. I tried to get it professionally cleaned once. They took one look at it and said no. Then they asked me to leave their forecourt, but the car wouldn't start because it was damp and it was French, and they had to push me down the road while I tried to bump start it and I only remembered to take the handbrake off when they had to ask more people to come out and help push.

Yup. There was no point blaming Helen. That much was clear. If this was about the Bearing Foods presentation, I was done for.

something about squirrels

'It's about the Bearing Foods presentation,' Trish said.

Nuts.

I tried not to shrug. I do a lot of shrugging. Especially when I'm about to get told off. I shrug at other times, too. Maybe it has something to do with hanging out in old French cars for so long.

Trish was wearing a cap sleeve shift dress with wide pink and white vertical stripes. She looked like a deckchair. A small deckchair. I could hear her blow-up cushion protesting as she squirmed in her chair and straightened to her full height. I could still barely see her over her laptop.

'I've just had Daniel Bearing on the phone,' she said.

Daniel Bearing was the CEO of Bearing Foods. We'd met, briefly.

'Yes?' I said.

No shrugging.

'He's not happy.' She said.

'I'm sorry to hear that.' I said.

Must not shrug.

'He said that there was some problem with the new Seedy-Pea-Nut-Slices?'

'Really?' I said.

I could feel my shoulders tighten and lift slightly.

'Something about squirrels,' she said.

'How odd,' I said.

Shrug averted. That was close. Now I just had to stop myself from smiling. Trish had drafted a policy document about smiling in the workplace. It was stuck on the wall in the kitchenette. In her view, smiling was the sign of an idle mind. She thought it looked unprofessional and insincere. She wanted her team to remain impassive and focused. She did her very best to lead by example. Apart from the whole wasp in the ear thing.

'I thought that Helen was helping you?' Trish said.

'Helen was great,' I said, suddenly aware that I shrug when I lie as well. Too late.

'Sort it out,' she said.

'I will,' I said.

And then I was dismissed.

I was glad. Trying not to shrug had really taken it out of me. I was exhausted.

G.I.T.S.

The Group Imaginative Thinking Session at Bearing Foods was not going well. Daniel Bearing's father didn't like the term 'brainstorming.' He thought it sounded outdated and silly. Group Imaginative Thinking Sessions were his idea. They happened once a week. It was part of his legacy. They also had an unfortunate acronym.

Daniel's father had recently retired and was now living in the Outer Hebrides in a former shooting lodge that had its own stone harbour and a beach of pure white sand and nine bedrooms and views to the Isle of Skye. He had worked hard for over thirty years so that he could live peacefully among puffins and grey seals and bottle-nosed dolphins in the middle of the North Atlantic. The constant buffeting of the wind was playing havoc with his hair implants.

Daniel was in charge now. He could call the weekly sessions anything he wanted to. He didn't really care one way or the other. Everyone just argued about the same things they always did. Mostly about cashews being too expensive and the laxative effect of eating too much coconut and whether chocolate chips really had any place in a low-fat snack bar.

Daniel Bearing wasn't really listening. He had a lot on his mind.

Dear Matilda

Just a quick note to let you know that washing machine No.76 arrived safely earlier today. How exciting. I doubt it will last any longer than the others, but it looks very fine in its cardboard overcoat. I haven't unpacked it yet. It's sitting in the middle of the living room at the moment. It seems happy enough. It has no idea what we have in store for it.

Mr Southerton (Jnr) has promised to come around tomorrow to plumb it in for me. Mr Southerton (Snr) is retiring. He says that he is too old to play around with hoses and stopcocks. He says his son is very good at fixing things. Much better than he is. Was. His son is called Bailey. He went to school with Jack. Do you know him? He has a very nice voice on the phone. He has also agreed to take the remains of washing machines No.74 and No.75 to the dump so that your father can park the car in the garage for a change. He won't. But he could.

Mr Southerton (Snr) says he will still call by and see Sidney when he is passing. I know that Sidney is very fond of his company.

Your brother is in South America somewhere. Don't ask me where. He did say, but you know what Jack is like when he starts talking about things that are blue. He gets all artistic and lyrical. I stopped listening in the end.

I have not heard from Katherine. I fear that the 'handbag

problem' may have flared up again. I will keep you posted.

Your father is at the Festival of Sand at Barmouth beach all week. He called and said there are seven dolphins already and he thinks there may be some mermaids arriving later. I fear another second place is on the cards.

Must dash. When are you coming to see us?

Love
Mum x

handbags

It was a patent leather top handle with a double zip and a detachable cross body strap. Katherine knew that she shouldn't stop and look. It was already too late. She had stopped. She had looked. She was drawn in. Her face was pressed against the glass.

It was sitting on its own acrylic plinth in the window of a shop that she was not allowed to enter. She was not banned. Katherine was always welcome inside. Cash or credit card. That was not the issue. She had made a promise. She had made the same promise before and been weak. Her resolve had not held. Not for long. She had given in after a month. Maybe a little less, but a month sounded better.

She had other top handle handbags of a similar design. Thirty or so. And three hundred different styles of handbag as well. In their own room. Lined up. On glass shelves. Constantly rearranged by size and colour and designer and season. That was a lot of handbags. That was why she had promised. So many times before. No more handbags. But this was different. This was something else. It was £485. It was worth it.

She tried to walk away but found herself walking towards the door of the shop instead. She couldn't stop herself. She went inside and was greeted like an old friend. She was weak. She knew it. She hated herself. But she bought the handbag anyway. She wanted it.

blue

Jack was lying in a tent near a small village in the palm swamps of an isolated area on the border of two South American countries. He had no idea which side of the border they were on. It didn't matter. He was floating a foot off the ground, and his toenails were talking to him. He had a fever. He was sweating. He was ice cold. He wasn't drinking enough water. He couldn't keep it down. He was hallucinating.

The nearest doctor was 80 miles away upriver. The journey would take six days. His guide assured him that the fever would break in 48 hours. He had seen it before. If it did not break in 48 hours, he would probably be dead. Either way, they weren't getting in the boat and traveling upriver to get a second opinion.

Jack was drifting in and out of consciousness. He did not mind. He had seen a Hyacinth Macaw in the wild. It had taken almost a week to reach the palm swamps on the edge of a border that had no real edges, only endless trees and muddy rivers.

Jack had seen the lurid blue of the Indigo Bunting, the pale blue of the Blue-Gray Gnatcatcher and the elegant blue of the

Purple Martin. The Hyacinth Macaw was another blue again. He was glad that he had traveled so far to see it. He would never forget.

He fell asleep. All his dreams were blue.

sand

Not sure that the nose is right.
Doesn't look right.
Looks wonky.
Askew.
Maybe it's just the direction of the sun?
Getting low now.
Sunset at 8.26pm.
Low sun.
That's all.
That's the problem.
Yeah.
It will look fine in the morning.
Stop messing with the nose.
You'll make it worse.
Move on.
Still got the tail to do.
Haven't even started on the tail.
Or the wings.
Going to be tricky.
Wrong sort of sand for wings.

29

Should have thought of that.
Why didn't I think of that?
Same thing last year.
Wrong sort of sand for porcupine quills.
Still got second place though.
Don't know how.
Idiot.
Sand sculpture of a porcupine?
Idiot.
What was I thinking?
Maybe if I used the plaque scaler again?
Add some more detail.
Won't notice it's wonky.
More scales.
Good thinking.
Useful having a dentist in the family.
Odd bloke though.
Wouldn't want to go on a camping holiday with him.
Get stuck in a tent.
Man has a thing against sand.
Odd bloke.
Doesn't know what he's missing.
Still looks wonky.
Not the sun then.
Bollocks.
Taken too much off the nose.
The nose is all wrong.
Don't think dragons have noses.
Snouts?

The Map of Us

Muzzles?
Doesn't really matter.
The nose is wrong.
Should have done a bloody dolphin.
Don't be an idiot.
Just do the nose right.
Can't.
Not enough sand.
Already taken too much off.
Off the nose.
Or the muzzle.
Snout.
Whatever it's called.
Have to start again.
Bollocks.
Idiot.
Don't have to start again.
Just make the whole thing smaller.
Done it before.
What time is high tide?
Should have done a bloody dolphin.
Idiot.

N

Abby was standing just inside the school gates. She had pen on her uniform. Asha Jackson did it. Abby didn't mind. Asha was her friend. They sat next to each other in class. Not all the time though. Sometimes she sat next to Francesca Drinkwater. She had long hair. Abby didn't have long hair. She had short hair. It was easier for her mum.

Abby was standing with a teacher. Abby didn't know what the teacher's name was. She was new. She wasn't really a teacher. Not yet. She was something else. Abby didn't know what.

Abby was getting bored of waiting. Everyone else had gone home. It was just her and the teacher that wasn't a teacher yet. Abby wanted to sit down. And something to drink.

Another teacher came out and told them both to come back inside. She said it like she didn't want Abby to hear, even though Abby was standing right there in front of her. She was called Mrs Whittle. She was the deputy headmistress.

Abby's mother wasn't coming to collect her.

Abby was six.

boots

At first Violet North sent her imaginary hero to sea, but it did not sit well with him. The blank expanse of blue water was not to his liking. The food was stale. His cabin was compact and stuffy. It was too near the engine room to sleep. The metal plates of the hull gathered condensation that seeped into his bunk. He shared the cabin with a fellow traveler who had bad dreams and tied his boots to his wrist so they would not be stolen. He could hear the cargo shifting. He worked his passage as far as the Azores and then disembarked, tired and disillusioned.

Violet offered him a better cabin, but he would not leave the comfort of the shore. She made him the Captain of a merchant ship. And a smuggler. And a retired Admiral. But he would not go. He found cheap lodgings and ate plump grilled sardines and drank green wine, and as the sun dipped he stood on the harbour wall and wondered what it was he would do next.

Violet sent off for a book to keep up with him. It was in Portuguese. Things could not continue this way.

She gave him boots. They were stolen from his companion

in the cabin. She had invented them. They were hers to steal. They did not fit, so she wrote that they were another size. That was better. He liked the boots more than he had liked the food onboard ship. He went for a walk to try them out.

oversight

Violet left him to walk in stolen boots for some time. She did not want a repeat of his disastrous voyage at sea. He was not turning out to be the man she had thought she imagined. Not at all. He had a mind of his own and a temperament that was combustible and a face she had not yet had the delicacy to finalise. His stride was long, and he had the hands of a violin player, or perhaps a pianist, and a voice that had not yet been tested. It was not until he had gone some several miles into an unwritten wasteland that she realised she had sent him on his way without a name. It was an oversight that she sought to quickly remedy.

Violet thought of her father, but his name would not do. He was a cruel man who had shunned her and stayed away and led a life elsewhere that did not include a daughter who could not walk far and whose frailty was a downright disappointment. She did not wish to recall his name. Or the name of her brother who pinched and pushed and kicked and dropped things from a height. Sharp things. Heavy things. Just because her legs did not work did not mean that she could not feel.

There were other names. Many. She wrote a list. And all the while a man with an uncertain face walked away from her into a shapeless void that had not yet been typed.

name

Violet's house had four floors and an attic. It was detached
and made of hard white bricks and was surrounded by a large
garden that was already beginning to look unkempt and
overgrown. There were 93 steps inside. The staircases were
narrow with painted banisters and fluted spindles. Some of
the spindles were broken or missing. The staircase from the
ground floor to the first floor was carpeted. The rest were
bare boards. The carpet was held in place by brass stair rods
made by Galbraith & Sons of Edinburgh. That would be his
name.

The washbasin in the first-floor bathroom was manufac-
tured by Arthur & Co. It sat on a cast iron stand and had a
white marble surround. There were 14 steps and a small landing
between the ground floor and the bathroom. It took Violet
five minutes to reach it. She clung to the banister. The paint
had worn off in places. There were many layers of paint hidden
beneath. Violet hoped to see them all one day. That would be
his name.

And so Arthur Galbraith was born. Not exactly born, but
brought into the world of imaginary existence. He was the

child of a brass stair rod and a first-floor washbasin with a marble surround. They represented the outer limits of Violet's universe. A name should mean something. His seemed apt somehow.

kissed

Violet had been thinking about Arthur Galbraith's face again, but she was yet to be convinced by any of the faces she had devised. None of them would do. She did not ask his opinion, for he had already shown himself to be difficult and ill-tempered when it came to making a choice.

Her problem was further complicated by a small technical matter. Almost every element of his face had an 'e' in it somewhere and the 'e' on her borrowed turquoise blue Royal Quiet Deluxe typewriter often stuck. There was an 'e' in 'nose' and 'ear.' There were two in 'eye' and 'eyebrows' and 'cheeks' and 'teeth' and 'forehead.' It was infuriating. Every time she would have to press a small button and the top of the Royal Quiet Deluxe typewriter would pop open automatically, making the interior of the machine accessible. Then she would unstick the 'e', replace the top, press the backspace key and start again.

Only Arthur's chin and mouth and lips were immune from the lengthy and annoying process. But they were not a place she cared to start. She knew something of chins and mouths, but a man's lips were unknown to her. She found herself thinking about them far more regularly than his nose. Did it matter what an imaginary explorer's lips looked like or felt like? She would never be kissed by such a man – and 'kissed' had an 'e' in it.

distance of paper

Violet set Arthur Galbraith to walk upon the Great Moor. It was a place of beauty and sadness and longing and hope and regret and joy, and it would take a lifetime to walk, for some things are not as simple as distance and direction.

Arthur put his boots to good use. They were no longer stolen. They were his. He had rock and peat and plain earth beneath his feet. He had a long stride, an unknown purpose and a Great Moor stood before him. Unexplored. Uncertain. A place without a map. He would be its pen.

And as he walked a face emerged. Not a face that Violet could have imagined. It was his face. It was his to choose. And strong hands not meant for instruments and a voice that said little that it did not mean.

The son of a brass stair rod and a washbasin finally appeared on a hilltop overlooking the Great Moor and looked south and east and north and west and decided to refuse the stars their steady counsel and let love guide him. He had a long road ahead. Not straight or flat or without discomfort.

And that is where Arthur and Violet and a turquoise blue Royal Quiet Deluxe typewriter began their journey together. Almost touching. Merely the distance of paper apart.

more sofa

Matt called the day after our meeting in the wine bar. The fate of the three-seater sofa was still preying on his mind. The whole 10.37am thing had rather overwhelmed the conversation.

'Hi,' he said. 'It's me.'

I knew who it was. We had been together for five years. Married for three. Just because we were separated now didn't mean that I would suddenly forget, even if I wanted to.

'Hi,' I said.

'Sorry about last night.'

'Yeah,' I said. I wanted to see where this was going before I said anything more definite.

'Are you busy?'

This was a typical Matt tactic. He liked to make sure that I was in the middle of doing something so that I'd have to stop doing it and give him my undivided attention. I made a mental note to find some way of quantifying his approach in a graph.

'Just stuff,' I said, trying not to be curt.

'I wanted to talk to you about the sofa,' he said.

'I know,' I said.

'How do you know?' He said.

'Because you always want to talk about it,' I said.

'Oh' he said. He sounded small and distant and brittle.

I sighed. I couldn't help it. This was getting ridiculous.

'You can have the sofa. Okay? I don't want it.' I said.

It was the truth.

There was a pause on the line.

'Why do you have to be such a bitch all the time,' he said.

Then he hung up.

half

We bought the three-seater sofa from a local secondhand furniture centre. It was hidden under a nest of tables and a glass-fronted display cabinet full of dog hair. It cost £55. I paid for it, and Matt said he would pay for his half when he got a full-time job. He had a full-time job for a while, but he didn't pay me back. We were still 92% in love back then, so I didn't mind that much. I minded when it suited me though. I used it against him sometimes. His unpaid half of the sofa had some value in a petty argument.

'You still haven't given me the money for your half of the sofa,' I'd say.

'Well I'll sit on the floor then!' he would say.

Then he would sit on the floor for about five minutes until he thought I'd calmed down. Then he would sneak back onto the sofa and hope that I hadn't noticed. I noticed. It was a victory of sorts.

The three-seater sofa was dusty pink. It was tired-looking. Grumpy even. The zips on the cushion covers were all broken. The arms were covered in coffee stains. At least that's what we hoped they were. It only had three casters. They were an unusual size that no one stocked anymore. We used a copy of 'Elementary Statistics and the Role of Randomness' to stop it from rocking backwards.

Matt liked to sleep on it in the afternoon when he was considering his future. He considered his future a lot. With his eyes closed. Gently snoring. He also got to sleep on it when our arguments weren't quite so petty. He didn't seem to mind. Matt and the grumpy pink sofa had some sort of connection that I didn't fully understand. I had never slept on the sofa. Why should I? I paid for the double bed as well.

dreams

I'm not sleeping. Not really. I sleep for an hour, then I wake up and listen. I'm not sure what I hope to hear. Breathing maybe. The bed feels wrong. Not empty so much as at the wrong angle. Too flat. I'm used to Matt being there. I told him we should have got a futon in the first place, but he didn't listen.

If I do get to sleep, I don't dream. Nothing. Not even fleeting glimpses. I have tried eating strong cheese before bed. And spicy food. It didn't work. Not in the way I hoped for anyway.

I miss dreaming. I used to dream. I don't know where my dreams have gone. I hope it's only a temporary thing. I hope they come back to me. Maybe they are unhappy, too? Maybe my dreams are having trouble adjusting?

I was going to draw a graph for the report, but I couldn't see the point. There was nothing to show.

sorry

Matt called back an hour later.

'Sorry,' he said.

I didn't say anything for a while.

That's when he hung up again.

Great.

We've been having a lot of conversations like that. Not really conversations. Single words followed by about a thousand miles of tense silence. 'Sorry' was fairly common. We've both said it. I've said it more. Not that I'm counting or anything.

We used to a talk a lot. Nothing profound. Just normal stuff. Endlessly.

I miss it and I don't.

Sometimes I wanted to talk about things that mattered to me. That didn't happen so often. That took preparation and timing. Maybe a takeaway. Or a rented DVD from the corner shop. And a bottle of wine. Always a bottle of wine. Or two.

I had to pay for the preparation. Sometimes it worked. I couldn't always make him listen though. That's where the timing came in. After the takeaway was normally too soon.

After the film had finished and Matt had watched all the special features and deleted scenes and alternate endings – that was my chance. After the bottle of wine was too late.

I don't buy as much wine now. Or takeaways. I haven't rented a DVD since he left.

I lied about the wine. I still buy about the same amount. I just get better wine, and it lasts a lot longer.

I'm getting used to the quiet. It's hard. I talk to myself. There's no one else.

rainbow

I decided early on that the centrepiece of my research would be a detailed questionnaire. It would be a paper-based document of as many pages as were necessary. I had a large lever arch folder to fill.

I knew that the answers to certain questions would carry more weight than others, so it would be subdivided into several different sections that I would score separately when it was complete.

I would call it 'The Compatibility Index.' It sounded great. I wrote it down on a piece of paper with a purple felt tip pen. It looked great, too. So I outlined it in yellow pen. Then I drew little green stars around the outline. Then I drew larger red stars around the green stars. Then I filled the space between the inner green stars and the outer red stars with small orange hearts. The I drew a rainbow in the background with all the wrong colours and realised I had probably gone too far. It was a mess. My brother was good with pens. I wasn't. Maybe I was being overly critical? I reminded myself that if Jack had drawn the same thing it would all be blue, including the rainbow, which would rather defeat the object.

I got out another piece of paper and wrote 'The Index' again, this time in ordinary pen. It looked room after you take down all the party decorations. It could not be helped. I punched some holes in the sheet of paper and clipped it inside the vast empty folder. That was even worse. Now it looked sad and lonely, like a room full of decorations when no one shows up to the party. I knew that feeling. I've had birthdays like that. Let's not go there.

I stuck the messy rainbow picture on the wall by my desk. The tape would probably tear the wallpaper off when I tried to take it down, but it didn't matter. It was my flat, and I didn't like it all that much anyway.

I liked the little orange hearts best. I went to get some chocolate. I was having fun already. Yeah. How hard could it be?

tortoise

I haven't always been good with numbers. For a long time, I had a disagreement with the numbers 3 and 5. They looked exactly the same to me. It sounds stupid. But however hard I looked I could not tell the difference between them. I tried. I practiced writing them down and always got them wrong. Reversed. Mirrored. Substituted one for the other. I wrote whole pages of perfectly formed numbers only to discover they were not the numbers I thought they were. My brother used to laugh at me. He was older. It was his job to laugh and point and call me names and make me the object of his ridicule. Jack wasn't good at numbers either. His disagreement ran much deeper. He had a problem with all of them. They were a foreign language to him.

Jack liked coloured pencils. I liked coloured pencils too, but I couldn't get them to do the things he could. He made coloured pencils sing. I made them squawk. He could do the same with felt pens and crayons and chalk and poster paint. He was rarely without colour. On his hands or face. Under his fingernails. On his clean shirt. If he could not find paper or a wall to draw on, he drew on his trousers. Every six months my parents had to buy a new washing machine. And more trousers. I liked trousers, too.

Katherine was not like us. Not ever. She liked dresses. With flowers. She brushed her hair and wore socks.

I failed exam after exam. Dates of important events muddled. Sums confused and incomplete. The world conspired against me. Everything had a 3 or a 5 in it. Or both.

Then one day it stopped. Just like that. 3 and 5 were suddenly not the same any more. They were different. Individual. Unique looking. I don't know how it happened. I was eleven. Nearly. I remember. It was the same day that Mr Everson from across the road backed his caravan over our tortoise. He said it was an accident. I don't know if the two things are linked somehow. I doubt there is a correlation. Nothing that I can prove now anyway.

view

Helen had been in my office again. I could tell. I don't leave traps or anything. That would be childish. I used to though. I could tell because there was a card waiting for me on my desk. It had 'I Am Sorry' written on it in silver glitter with a picture of a sad hamster holding a wilting daisy. It wasn't signed. I knew it was from Helen. She left the price on the back.

Helen and I have a love hate relationship that is heavily skewed towards the loathe and detest end of the spectrum. Apparently I have a better office than her. It has a window that overlooks the canal. The canal is a toxic slick of greeny-brown water full of traffic cones and paper coffee cups, topped with a thick layer of oily scum. Occasionally a rat will float by. On its back. Legs in the air. Usually with another rat trying to eat it. Or mate with it. It's hard to tell. Helen's window looks out over the allocated parking in front of the building and the main road. Somehow my view is superior.

Helen likes to 'borrow' my things and leave them on her desk in plain sight - daring me to come and reclaim them. Proving ownership of a stapler can be a difficult and time-consuming process. Now she has begun to write her name on the bottom of things that don't belong to her.

So have I. She uses a marker pen. I have a UV security pen that can't be seen under normal light. I may have written something rude about her on the bottom of my desk organiser. I know it will be her next target. She can't lift my filing cabinet.

64.726%

Helen has been where I am now. Twice. I would have expected her to be more understanding. She still has both of her wedding rings. And a tattoo. I haven't seen it. I've heard about it though. Apparently it says something about undying love with a heart in the background and some poorly drawn butterflies. Romantic. Only one problem. To my knowledge, she was never married to anyone called Derek.

Her first marriage lasted an impressive nine days. The argument started at the reception. It escalated during the taxi ride to the airport. They were asked to leave the Executive Departure Lounge when other passengers complained about the shouting. Free champagne on the flight calmed things down, but it was only a temporary reprieve. It all kicked off again when they reached the hotel. They didn't even make it to the end of their honeymoon. Her husband flew home early with a budget airline and got diverted to Stockholm. Helen decided to stay behind. The resort was all-inclusive, with three vast swimming pools and an attractive bar manager with taut abdominal muscles.

Helen's second marriage lasted a little longer. I am not sure how. The pair lived entirely separate lives from around the third month. He came to one office party, but we weren't sure who he was, so no one talked to him, least of all his wife.

By the time she was twenty-eight, Helen had been a Mrs Drake and a Mrs Cortes. Now she is using her maiden name again. Miss Cook. The sign on her door just says 'Helen.' It was easier for everyone to remember.

In case you were wondering, the average marriage lasts around 8 years. Not an exact figure. 64.726% was therefore an approximation based on limited data. Here is how I worked it out:

$$(y1 - x1) + (y2 - x2) = z$$
$$(z \times 8 \times 365)/100 = 64.726\%$$

But that isn't why it's funny. It's a statistics joke. It's funny because it's accurate to three decimal places. See?

I don't know why I bother.

same

Daniel Bearing had seven identical suits. They were grey. And seven identical ties. They were black. And seven identical shirts. They were white. They hung in a row in a purpose built, humidity-controlled wardrobe on identical hand crafted wooden coat hangers. They were Italian walnut. He had seven identical pairs of shoes. They were handmade black wingtip Oxfords.

Daniel had a nice car and a nice apartment in a nice area and nice neighbours and absolutely no social life because he was never at home.

Daniel worked for twelve hours a day, six days a week and only took a holiday when he was told to. He lived alone. He was too busy to live with anyone else. They would never see him. They would never notice he had been and gone because all his clothes were identical.

Daniel's life was a carbon copy of his father's. His father had worked for over thirty years to build Bearing Foods into an award-winning company with an annual turnover in the millions.

Daniel didn't have to think for himself. It had all been done for him. Right down to the colour of his socks. They were grey. Like his suits.

Daniel Bearing knew one thing though. He didn't want to end up on a puffin-infested island wearing a hat like his father.

Dear Matilda

Just a quick note to say that washing machine No.76 has settled in nicely and is behaving itself – so far. Bailey Southerton did an excellent job of installing it. He turned up as arranged and was not what I expected at all. He has mended some other things around the house, too. And he found the lawnmower. He has taken it away as it requires new parts and a full service. He says he might even have some wooden spindles to replace the ones on the staircase that are broken or missing. Bailey Southerton really is a very nice young man. I think you will like him. Mr Southerton (Snr) sends his best regards.

Sidney is recovering from a bad cold. He is asleep under the apple tree in the garden as I write this. He does so love the garden. Despite his illness, he could not be persuaded to stay in bed this one time. He was overjoyed to hear that Bailey might be able to fix the lawnmower. He remembers the garden how it was when your grandfather was alive.

Your brother is back from his trip to South America but has now flown to Italy, where he is working with a cosmetics company who are looking for a new blue. I didn't think there was a such a thing as a 'new blue,' but Jack feels confident that he will be able to come up with something that they haven't seen before. He started talking about wavelengths and nanometres and the optical spectrum of visible light again. That's when I stopped listening.

Katherine is buying handbags again. Oh dear.

The Map of Us

Your father will be at the 3rd Annual Sand-athon at Cabthorne beach all weekend. He has high hopes this time. I'm fairly certain he will be disappointed. Bloody dolphins! Washing machine No.76 will have its first real test on his return. We would all love to see you.

Love
Mum x

5 things about washing machines

Washing machines usually lasted about six months in our house. The abrasive nature of sand saw to that. My father's clothes were always full of it. There was a well-established pre-wash ritual of pocket emptying and shaking and leaving things out to dry and more shaking and rinsing, but it didn't seem to make a lot of difference. After six months, something would always snap or disintegrate or crack, and we would have to buy another washing machine to take the place of the one in the kitchen that was in pieces.

Whenever we needed a new washing machine, everyone always blamed Jack. It was tradition. His pen- and paint- and crayon-covered trousers were bad at times, but it wasn't his fault. We blamed Jack because it made him happy. He was intensely proud of destroying so many innocent washing machines. It was the highlight of his childhood.

We started giving the washing machines names, but that just made it harder when they inevitably broke and had to get taken to the tip. I cried for a week when Marjorie was carted away. Everyone was glad to see the back of Graham.

The record for the longest lasting washing machine was held by Desmond at eight months and two days. On the third day of the eighth month, Desmond burst into flames in the middle of a cotton cycle. Something to do with the heating element getting covered in fluff. We blamed Jack, as usual.

All our washing machines were supplied and installed by Mr Bill Southerton of 'Southerton's Electrical Appliances' in the village. He was glad of the regular trade. He paid off his mortgage, went on two holidays a year and paid for his own hip replacement. We got a 15% discount.

free coffee

Jack did not look like a world authority on the colour blue. Everyone said that. At first. They doubted him. They kept him waiting in the lobby. They asked him if he wanted tea or coffee or chilled water, and then they left him sitting there for half an hour while they checked his credentials rigorously. They secretly called other companies he had worked for in the past and asked for a detailed description. They all said the same thing.

'He's about six-foot-tall with long hair and he wears jeans and faded T-shirts and he looks nothing like a world authority on the colour blue. He looks like he just left his skateboard outside and came in for free coffee.'

That set alarm bells ringing. Sometimes they got security to check for skateboards.

'Is he really a world authority on the colour blue?' Would be the next question.

'Yes,' would be the answer.

'Okay. Thanks for your time. Sorry to bother you,' they would say and put the phone down.

Then they would apologise for keeping him waiting in the

lobby for so long, and Jack would joke with them that he was used to it and it happened all the time.

On the way to the meeting they would always ask him why it was that he favoured blue over any other colour.

And Jack would smile.

'It was the colour of my grandmother's typewriter,' he would say.

agreement

Katherine thought that she might be able to sneak the top handle handbag into the house without her husband seeing. She was wrong. Clive was home early. His 5.15 had cancelled. Clive was a dentist who had scrupulously clean hands and very small eyes that were worryingly close together. He was a good man who enjoyed drilling holes in people's faces. He was a contradiction.

Katherine and Clive lived in a modern and minimalist house where visitors were welcome as long as they took their shoes off in the hall and washed their hands before touching anything. It was painted throughout in shades of white. It all looked the same white, but all the whites were actually infinitesimally different. It was a subtle effect. Some of the walls looked slightly dirtier than others, but you had to look really closely.

Clive was sitting on the white stairs when Katherine walked through the white door and took her shoes off in the white hallway. There was really no way she could hide the patent leather handbag that was wrapped in tissue paper inside the carrier bag that had 'Exclusive Handbags' written on the side in big letters. Clive pinched the skin between his eyebrows. There wasn't much to pinch. Katherine knew what it meant.

'I thought we had an agreement,' he said.

'I know,' she said.

'You were doing so well,' he said.

'I know,' she said.

'Then why?' he said.

'Because it's perfect.'

Clive laughed. Not a cruel laugh or an amused laugh but a laugh that was full of inevitability and surrender.

'No handbag is perfect,' he said.

'Don't say that,' she said, suddenly close to tears.

'I love you,' he said, softly.

'I know,' she said. Then she left him sitting on the stairs while she went to find a place on a glass shelf for her new handbag.

more sand

It's going to break off.
I'm telling you.
Wind keeps up like this it's going to break off.
Dry out.
Crumble.
The whole thing.
Break off.
Nice idea.
Too ambitious.
Wrong sort of sand for ambitious.
This is play-it-safe sand.
Saw it as soon as I got out of the car.
Don't-take-any-chances sand.
Not the right sort of sand for a giraffe.
A sand sculpture of a giraffe?
Idiot.
What was I thinking?
Be fine.
Be extra careful.
Soft brushes.

Small tools.
Grain at a time stuff.
Big things.
Giraffes.
Take longer.
That's all.
You can do it.
Three hours left.
Delicate touch.
Spray bottle.
Not too much.
A mist.
You can win.
Beat the dolphins with a giraffe.
See their faces then.
I miss her.
Try not to think about it.
Think about the giraffe.
I miss her.
Giraffe.
I miss the sound of that stupid typewriter.
The look on their faces.
I miss the sound of her breathing next to me.
Don't.
I miss everything about her.
Stop.
Stop now.
Don't want to forget.
She's gone.

It's going to break off.
I'm telling you.
Wind keeps up like this.
Crumble.
Everything does.
You can do it.
Steady hand.
Be gentle.
Grain at a time stuff.
Look.
Over there.
Dolphin.
Dorsal fin has gone.
Broken off.
Told you.
Still in it.
Still got a chance.
Giraffe?
Idiot.
I miss her.

NE

Abby was waiting in Mrs Whittle's office. She was sitting in the green chair in front of Mrs Whittle's desk where you sat when you had done something wrong. Abby hadn't done anything wrong. Not that she could remember. She had pen on her uniform, but you couldn't get told off for that. It wasn't bad pen. It looked like a fish. Or a balloon. You could hardly see it.

Mrs Whittle was talking outside in the corridor. Abby didn't know who she was talking to. The other teacher had gone home. The teacher that was still learning to be a teacher. She had nice hair and a fringe. She had funny teeth though. Abby wanted a fringe. She couldn't have one. Her hair was too short. It was easier for her mum.

Abby was alone in the room. She wanted to go home. It was 5.18pm. There was a clock on the wall behind the desk. It didn't make any sound.

Mrs Whittle stopped talking. Abby heard her walking away down the corridor. She was with someone. Abby didn't know who. She couldn't see. The door was pulled to.

The school was empty. Abby didn't like it. She wanted her mum to come and collect her. Her mum didn't. Someone else did.

date night

It was 8.35pm. The bar wasn't exactly packed. It was snowing outside. Not the kind of snow that can make even a disreputable old city like London look picturesque, but the other kind that quickly turns into a grey mush and leaves a ragged tidemark on your shoes that is almost impossible to get out. That kind. The singles event was supposed to have started an hour ago. Matt had been told that it was always busy. Every Wednesday night. Except this one. Clearly anyone with any sense had stayed at home and saved their shoes for another day.

There were a few people milling around. Maybe about forty in total. Mostly middle-aged men with unbuttoned suit jackets and thinning hair. They were all sucking their guts in and looking at the door. He wondered how long it would be before one of them passed out. Matt hoped he wouldn't end up like them.

There were a few single women, too. One was wearing a chunky sweater that had one arm longer than the other and looked like it had been knitted by a chimpanzee. The other appeared to have a chandelier hanging from her nose. It caught the light in a strange way and sent a shower of sparkles dancing across the ceiling.

Matt had never been to the bar before. It was new. A few months ago it had been a trendy seafood restaurant, and before that it was a trendy delicatessen. Now it was a trendy bar that was practically empty. Matt was drinking a glass of tap water with ice and a slice of lime. He was drinking it like it was a gin and tonic. It was much, much cheaper to pretend.

Matt had come a long way. He thought he'd better make some kind of effort. There was a woman sitting next to him on a stool. She had short red hair and freckles. She looked like trouble.

'Hi,' Matt said.

'Hello,' the woman with the red hair said back.

'I'm Matt,' he said.

'Yes. I know,' she said.

Matt looked confused.

'Do I know you?'

'I don't think so,' she said, smiling. 'It's written on your name badge.'

'Oh,' Matt said, suddenly feeling like a dropped ice-cream. 'Yeah. I forgot.'

'First time?' she said. It was a statement more than a direct question.

'Yeah. Something like that. How about you?'

'I've been coming for a couple of months,' she said, sipping her drink. It was probably a real gin and tonic. Matt could see the bubbles.

'Months?' Matt said.

'What can I say? I'm picky. I've made mistakes in the past.'

'Me too,' he said.

The woman with the real gin and tonic and the red hair and freckles turned towards him.

'Are you married?' she said. There was a hint of disquiet and suspicion in her voice.

'I was,' Matt said.

'Divorced?'

'Separated.'

'Not quite divorced then,' she said. Her smile was thin.

'Getting divorced.'

'How's that going?'

'We're sorting through some stuff. Arguing over a sofa mostly.'

'A sofa?'

'Yeah. Sounds stupid, doesn't it?'

'A little,' she said. Then her face softened. 'What do I know? I'm here too, right?'

'And you?' he asked.

'Unexpectedly single. It happens. I just never thought it would happen to me.'

Matt looked into his drink and hoped she didn't notice it was tap water.

'This is kind of scary. It's been a while.'

'You'll be fine,' she said. 'You'll soon get to know everyone. Just watch out for Gretchen in the hand knitted jumper. Oh, and Tabitha with the dangly nose ring. She's a little intense. Whatever you do, don't mention astrology.'

'I'll try not to.'

'And Lindsey isn't here yet. She's always late. She collects china elephants. If you don't like china elephants, I really wouldn't bother talking to her. She's lovely though. So, if you do like china elephants, you're in luck. Have a great night.'

The woman with the red hair got up and started to walk away.

'Nice meeting you,' Matt said.

'You too. Best of luck with the sofa thing.'

'Thanks. I didn't catch your name.'

'It's on my badge,' she said, turning back so that he could read the large white label that had been staring him in the face the whole time.

'Charlotte?' he said.

'Yeah.'

'Maybe see you later then?'

'Maybe,' she said, and then she was gone.

special friend

The turquoise blue Royal Deluxe typewriter was fast becoming Violet's dearest friend. They spent most of each day together.

It came in a hard case with a key on a piece of string and a black plastic handle and an instruction booklet inside. The instruction booklet had helpful touch-typing exercises in the back. Violet ignored those. She typed slowly and deliberately using only the middle fingers of each hand. She made small fists with the rest, locked in place by her thumbs. It served her well enough, and she was in no hurry. Arthur Galbraith could wait.

She typed on both sides of the paper. It seemed wasteful for her to do otherwise. She had to send off for it and it was expensive and it arrived wrapped in waxed paper and there were only 80 watermarked sheets in each pack. She had a choice to make – 80 pages single-sided or 160 pages double-sided. Violet knew the value of thrift. She was by now twenty-seven years of age and had her own house with a large garden, and she had already sold most of the good furniture to get by.

The typewriter had many special features that she did not

fully understand. The right-hand margin warning bell was fairly self-explanatory. It also had a Variable Line Spacer and a Magic Margin Button and a Speed Selector and a Touch Control that adjusted the sensitivity of the keys. Violet was not impressed by any of it. The typewriter was turquoise blue. That was what made it special.

title

title

Arthur Galbraith's adventures were to be written in the form of walking guides. As she seldom left her own house, Violet considered a walking guide to be much like a cookery book – they were bought to be looked at and not to be followed. But she was eager to avoid being called a charlatan or a fraud, even though that was exactly what she had it in her mind to become. She did not want her readers to find themselves lost.

She immediately removed Arthur Galbraith from the present and placed him on the Great Moor some distance in the past. If any person should set about to walk in Arthur's footsteps believing the landscape he traversed was real, they would find it much altered and assume that the passage of time was to blame for erasing the landmarks and byways that were described in such detail in the book.

To further confuse people, Violet decided to accompany the text with a series of rudimentary pen and ink sketches that were so general and imprecise that they offered the walker no help at all in identifying where they were or what it was they had the intention of traveling towards. Places that only had shape and colour and substance in the thoughts of a lonely young woman sitting at a borrowed typewriter, trapped in a house with a large and untidy garden.

Violet would call the book *Galbraith's Boot*. She chose the title for one simple reason: it did not contain a troublesome 'e.'

volume one

The first volume of *Galbraith's Boot,* entitled 'Walks from Shiny Brook to Burton Hole,' was published in 1961 when Violet was twenty-eight. It purported to be a reprint of the original edition from 1897, written by Arthur Galbraith himself and illustrated by his own hand in a notebook that he carried for such a purpose. It was, of course, a lie. All of it. There was nothing printed on any page that was not a fiction or a clever deceit of some kind.

It was a walking guide written by a woman who could not walk far, writing as a man who had died four decades earlier and only ever existed in her imagination. It proved to be surprisingly popular.

The first volume was a small, pocket-sized book, bound in cheap board. It sold out in a fortnight and was reprinted several times thereafter. A second volume, 'Walks from Black Lake to Tin Gate Mire,' appeared a few months later and did much the same.

Violet North purchased the Royal Quiet Deluxe typewriter from her neighbour with her first royalties and bought for it a new carbon ribbon and a great deal of paper. She settled down to write, little realising the momentous upheaval she would cause. The Great Moor was stirring.

praise for
Galbraith's Boot

The foremost book on the Great Moor. Full of atmosphere and sly wit.

John Wallace Dobson.
Curator of Diairies & Journals
British Library

Arthur Galbraith was a pioneer and a visionary.

Edgar Mant
Monthly Gazette of Walking

Authentic and comprehensive. An unmatched work of topographical genius.

Joyce Scoines
Chief Cartographer
The Admiralty

Jules Preston

A much sought-after guide for the intrepid walker and amateur explorer alike.

Sir Evelyn Stevens
Explorer

A gifted artist and a fearless author.

Barbara Atkins

Arthur Galbraith's fine illustrations remind me of places that I visited often as a child. He was a remarkable fellow, and I feel honoured and fortunate to have called him my friend.

William Bell
Broadcaster

drawn

Violet considered drawing her sketches of the Great Moor in the garden.

The garden was large. A little more than an acre. Violet knew what it looked like from her window on the first floor. She thought that it was beautiful, but she did not go there. Not anymore. She was afraid. Inside was bad enough. They had put her out in the sun when she was younger. Put her out in the sun in the garden and left her there. Fresh air and sun would be good for her. Good for her bones. Make her strong. Get her out of the way.

Some nights they forgot to bring her in. Some nights it was something other than forgetting.

Violet drew her sketches in the front parlour or sitting on the stairs instead.

85

5 things about the garden

The garden had walls on three sides made from the same hard white brick as the house and topped with cement and tall shards of broken glass. The house occupied the fourth side of the square and was connected to the wall by a wrought iron fence that needed painting. Honeysuckle and wisteria and clematis and ivy covered the walls and the rusting fence and the house and some of the upper floor windows too. No one looked out of those.

The garden once had several circular lawns connected by gravel paths. And a glasshouse and a potting shed and flower beds and shaped hedges and pears and peaches trained against the south-facing wall and an apple tree and a compost heap and a belief in itself that had since been sorely shaken.

The lawns were gone. The paths were overrun. The glasshouse looked like a pond of broken ice. The potting shed was hidden beneath brambles and stinging nettles. Honeysuckle and wisteria and clematis and ivy had strangled the pears and peaches. The apple tree was the home of wasps. It was not the garden's fault. The garden had done its best to survive. Just as Violet had.

The garden was lonely and heartbroken. It wanted so much to please her. It knew that she was frightened. It wanted to help, but it could not. It could not do it on its own.

The garden was patient. As all gardens are. As they have to be. Violet watched it from her window, and the garden tried to say to her 'forgive me,' but it was only a garden, and it could not speak. Instead it waited. There was still time.

music question

'What music do you like?' I said.

It was one of those meaningless questions you ask someone when you don't know what else to say because you haven't really spoken to them before and you're building up to a kiss, but you haven't quite got there yet even though you both clearly want to.

'Jazz,' he said.

'Okay,' I said, because I was still interested in the kissing part and this was only a minor setback that I hadn't really anticipated because Matt sometimes wore a tie.

I should have known then that our marriage would falter, at least in some small part, due to musical differences. But we hadn't even kissed at that point and I was feeling optimistic about the future even though the future would be dominated by a lever arch file full of diagrams and statistics that showed exactly how and why we failed and why we were both alone again.

For now, though, we were on a beach and I was absorbing the fact that Matt liked jazz and that there were so many other things I would learn about him in the days and years ahead, including the fact that we were not really made for each other after all.

The light was beginning to fade. He held my hand as we walked back towards my old estate car that may or may not start because it was French and full of sand.

'I like Country,' I said, in the spirit of sharing.

'Oh,' he said.

The world trembled a little. The kissing was still there somewhere on the horizon, but I could feel that it had moved inexplicably further away. I should have known.

Lazy Mo

Openness is obviously a huge part of any successful relationship. A basic level of honesty.

Matt said that he liked jazz. That was bad enough. What he failed to mention was that he preferred experimental jazz.

He failed to mention it until well after the kissing had actually happened. He didn't say a word before kissing had turned in to clothes being removed. The slow, romantic clothes-removing stage passed, and still nothing. The quick and less romantic but more location specific clothes-removing stage followed without any further reference to jazz at all. Then we decided to move in together, and jazz became a major talking point almost immediately.

Matt liked to listen to pioneering albums that were full of toots and screeches. Complex and lengthy compositions that lacked any overarching harmonic structure and described a new and progressive musical language by doing things with trumpets and saxophones that didn't sound entirely wholesome. That's what he said. The first part anyway.

Matt spent days rearranging the furniture in the living room to achieve the best stereo image for his speakers. He cancelled out unwanted audio reflections by moving my favourite books from the bookshelf to the mantlepiece over the fire. He wanted to cover the walls in empty egg boxes, but I said no. He said if he sprayed them with grey paint they would look exactly like commercially available acoustic tiles but at the fraction of the cost. I said no. He collected the egg boxes anyway. He went to all this effort just so he could listen to music that sounded like an instrument salesman being pushed down a flight of concrete stairs wearing trousers made of trombones.

Matt had a jazz face, too. Inscrutable. Eyes tightly shut. Head slightly lolling. Tapping along with his hand on his knee. Fingers occasionally playing along on an imaginary piano. I often left the room and had a good laugh at his expense. The joke soon wore thin.

I was not allowed to play any Country on his system. Ever. Even when he was out. It would somehow degrade the purity of the momentous clatter of the Lazy Mo Trio or the Chet Pearlman Band.

Towards the end I used to play my favourite Country tapes in the car just to annoy him.

blueberry

Helen was looking smug. More than usual. The last time she looked that pleased with herself she had just stolen my hole punch in an audacious lunchtime raid. I knew it was safely locked in my desk drawer, so it couldn't be that.

She was waiting for me by the water cooler. She does that a lot. It's annoying, but sometimes I like to veer away at the last minute and go to the toilets instead. One day she'll get wise. But it isn't as easy to wait outside the toilets for someone without attracting attention.

I needed water more than I needed to go to the toilet, so I was forced to confront Helen and find out what it was she was feeling so self-satisfied about. I didn't need to ask.

'I have just managed to secure the services of one of the foremost experts in the field of colour theory,' she said, downing her water in one and crushing the paper cup in her hand triumphantly before throwing it at the bin and missing. It skittered off across the floor. She followed it with her eyes but only until it went under the photocopier, at which point she clearly decided it was someone else's responsibility.

I knew what she was talking about. It was one of her

projects. The development of a new blackcurrant and blueberry flavoured smoothie that had been stalled for weeks. The manufacturers couldn't find the right shade of blue for the product. They had considered purple as an alternative, but they were hoping to target the younger consumer who reacted positively to a strong blue. Something that looked like shower gel or a disinfectant that you wipe on wounds to stop gangrene setting in.

'Congratulations,' I said as flatly as I could without sounding sarcastic. I think I gauged it pretty well.

'Thanks,' she said. 'He's a blue specialist. He works all over the world.'

Suddenly I knew where this was going.

'He's flying in tomorrow to meet the team,' she said. 'He's called Jack Eastleigh.'

My brother.

reminder

Helen never knew me before I was married. Before I became Mrs Matilda Westicott. She had no idea that Jack Eastleigh was my older brother. I don't keep photographs of my family on my desk or anywhere else in my office. There are several reasons for this.

There are few pictures of us all together - and none that I am fond of. My father was always on a beach somewhere with his trowels and dental instruments. My mother was working on my grandmother's books. My sister had to stand in the middle and be allowed to go off and change her dress. My brother was always covered in pen or crayon, or paint, or chalk, or a combination of all four. I looked like a smaller version of my brother. In his faded hand-me-down dungarees that were covered in his drawings. The ones that wouldn't wash out because the washing machine was nearly broken.

I do have a few personal items. I have a picture of a rose garden modeled in sand. It took my father three days to complete. It was for a competition. He came second behind a pod of cartoon dolphins. He won a silver-plated trophy featuring a bucket and spade and a cheque for £50. Dolphins always won, but my father refused to have anything to do with them and settled for coming second all the time instead.

I have all 16 volumes of *Galbraith's Boot* lined up along the window sill. I like to look at them. They remind me of my grandmother and my mother and of love.

coincidence

Jack was sitting in Business Class. The plane was delayed on the runway, but the captain had just made an announcement and sounded relaxed about it and promised to get everyone to their destination on time even if he had to get out and push. Jack had heard the joke before, but it still made an impression on the corners of his eyes. It didn't get any further than that.

Jack had plenty of legroom and two windows and a slide out table for his drawing pad and a glass of champagne that he didn't really want. He was going to let it go warm and flat and see how long it took the cabin crew to notice. He opened his specially made tin. Inside the specially made tin there were 45 specially made pencils. All of them were blue. 45 different kinds of blue. He chose one. It was blue. He started to draw on his pad.

The lady in the seat across the aisle had been watching.

'Are you in the right seat?' She said.

'I believe so,' Jack said, picking another pencil and continuing to draw. It was blue.

'If you don't mind me saying - you don't look like you are in the right seat,' she continued.

Jack smiled.

'I get that a lot,' he said. 'It happens all the time. Especially at work.'

'And what is it that you do?' She asked. It was more of an accusation.

'I'm a world authority on the colour blue,' Jack said, showing her the drawing on the pad. It was mainly pale blue with some other blue that wasn't so pale.

'Oh. What a coincidence, the woman said. 'I'm a world authority on the colour yellow.'

'You're joking?' Jack said, suddenly interested.

'You started it,' the woman said, turning away and putting her headphones on.

5 things about Jack

Jack was a world authority on the colour blue. He travelled the world constantly. He had no real home. He stayed with friends. Slept on couches.

Jack was a world authority on the colour blue. He was unmarried. Unattached. It was not for lack of commitment or courage or opportunity. He travelled the world. Slept on couches. Had no real home. That was the sum total of it.

Jack was a world authority on the colour blue, but he was normal and easy-going and good company and funny and disarming and fallible. He had no real home and many friends throughout the world with comfortable couches.

Jack was a world authority on the colour blue, but he tried not to talk about it all the time. Jack knew that everything and everywhere was basically muddy coloured and that blue was a narrow path that he could follow without distraction and still see more of the world because of it.

Jack was not the only world authority on the colour blue. There were others. Professor Raymond Shand was an American whose work focused primarily on the synthetic indigo dyes used in the plastics industry. Kelly Garcia was an avid collector of azurite and rarely left the copper mines in Namibia. And then there was Nadia Danti. She was an expert art conservator specialising in the restoration of 14th and 15th century paintings using only natural ultramarine. Her family originally came from Afghanistan where they had traded in lapis lazuli for more than a thousand years. Blue was in her blood. Jack and Nadia had never met. But they were about to.

yes

Jack felt someone tap him lightly on the shoulder. He turned in his seat. A woman was standing in the aisle. She smiled.

'I couldn't help overhearing your conversation,' she said.

'Yes,' Jack said stupidly. He wanted to say so much more but found that he could not. Something was no longer under his command. Something was acting on its own. Something had hung a 'Closed' sign on the door to his brain and poured hot wax into his heart.

'You must be Jack Eastleigh,' the woman said.

'Yes,' Jack said even more dimly than before. His hands were suddenly cold.

'My name is Nadia Danti,' she said.

'I know,' Jack said.

And that was all it took.

Actually, the smile was all it took.

The rest was just introductions.

What had happened had already happened.

It had started over a thousand years before.

new arrivals

I agreed to pick Jack up from the airport. Helen thought she had talked me into it, but I didn't take much persuading. I took *some* persuading though, otherwise she would have wondered what was going on. Helen isn't as stupid as she looks, but it's a pretty close-run thing.

I was late. My old estate car full of sand isn't quite as agile as it used to be. And it's French. And it was early in the morning. And it was damp. And it doesn't like to start when it's damp. And it overheats if you drive at over 70mph, which you shouldn't because it's breaking the law even if you are late to pick up your brother from the airport and you haven't seen him for over six months because he's an important figure in the study and commercial application of the colour blue.

By the time I arrived and found somewhere to park and paid a stupid amount to park there, his flight had landed. I ran through the terminal building. That makes me sound super sporty or something. I didn't run all the way. Not in one go. I did some fast walking and some stopping to get my breath back, too.

I could see Jack waiting by the arrivals gate, despite the

sweat dripping into my eyes and misting up my driving glasses. He was talking to someone. They were standing so close to each other that they were almost touching. I was shocked. I had never seen my brother in love before.

trumps

I offered to give Nadia a lift. I could hear the pair of them talking in the back as we drove towards her house.

'I use 5 litre cans of specially mixed paint,' Jack said.

'I use a pigment made from powdered lapis lazuli and oil,' Nadia said. 'I have it made for me in Venice by Mr Marcelino Pio-Padovese. He is 103 years old. His family have been making natural ultramarine since 1598. They are one of only four companies in the world that still do.'

'Oh,' said Jack. 'I use a 9-inch roller or a 4-inch brush. My last collection of six canvases took me half an hour to complete.'

'Each?' Nadia asked.

'All six,' Jack said.

'Oh,' Nadia said. 'The last piece I worked on was a panel by Vasco Salvatore Boccamazza entitled 'Virgin in the Garden' painted in 1510. I had an area of the Virgin's cloak to retouch. The damaged area was less than an inch square. I had to wear a magnifying visor with its own illumination as I was working in a vault in the basement of a museum in Switzerland. I sat on a scaffold and had the piece on a hydraulically controlled easel. It took me eight months.'

'Oh,' Jack said.

I turned left into a wide street of tall red brick buildings. 'Where can I drop you off?' I said.

'Anywhere around here,' Nadia said.

'Can I stay on your couch?' Jack said.

'Yes,' Nadia said.

Then they both got out and I didn't see him again for days.

start

Start.
Start.
Start.
Don't start then.
See if I care.
Bloody car.
Start.
Don't start.
Right.
Okay.
It's okay.
Breathe.
Give it a minute.
Give it a minute to think about it.
Give it a minute.
It's French.
It's old.
It's raining.
It's having a moment.
That's all.

Jules Preston

Start.
Staaaart.
Staaaaaaaaaaaaaaaaaart.
Start.
Don't start.
Flooded it now.
Idiot.
Should've waited.
Put it in first.
Clutch down.
Next time.
Catch it by surprise.
What's that in French?
Surprise.
The same.
Sounds better in French.
Have I got everything?
Buckets?
Tools?
Second Place trophy?
Dark by the time I get home.
Empty.
Silent.
I miss her.
And that stupid blue typewriter.
Kids.
Laughter.
'Beaten again dad?'
Tilly.

'Yeah.'
'Dolphins, dad'?
Jack.
'Yeah. What do we say?'
'Bloody dolphins!'
Everyone shouting together.
Laughter.
Dancing about.
Even Katherine.
Miss it all.
Complaints.
Sand in the sink.
Sand on the stairs.
Sand everywhere.
Need a new washing machine.
Full of sand.
Okay.
Again.
Okay.
Blame Jack.
He loves it.
Look at his face.
Makes him feel special.
Covered in pen.
Face under there somewhere.
Sell his trousers to pay for it.
State of them.
Clean yesterday.
New last week.

Modern art.
Make a print of his face.
Every day.
Lines.
Circles.
Make him blow his nose first.
Never grow up.
Can't stop them.
Grew up.
Left.
I miss them.
Start.
Thanks.
Wasn't so hard.
What was all the fuss about?
Time to go.
Time to go back.
If only.
If only I could.

party

It was Daniel Bearing's birthday. He was thirty. He was alone in his nice apartment. He received one card. It had a puffin on it.

It was late. His nice neighbours were having a party. It wasn't for him. He wasn't invited. They didn't think to invite him. What was the point? He was never there. The one time they did invite him he turned up in a grey suit and tie. They were sure they wrote 'casual' on the invitation. And 'bring a bottle.' He bought a box of low-fat snack bars. Frankly they were glad he wasn't home very often.

Daniel tried his answer machine. There were no messages. There were never any messages. No one called him at home. What was the point? He was never there.

Daniel sat on one of two identical leather couches and put the card on the designer glass-topped table that was so heavy they had to lift it through the window with a crane.

He heard the sound of laughter and friends and music and idle conversation coming through the walls. He could feel unhappiness bubbling up inside him.

tired

Daniel Bearing was tired. He was tired of lactose intolerance and nut allergies and choking hazards and coeliacs and vegans and people with poorly fitting dentures and complaints about the number of cherries and non-recyclable cellophane wrappers and everything having the visual appeal of a squirrel turd.

He was tired of yoghurt covered bars and goji berries and puffed brown rice and Group Imaginative Thinking Sessions and the endless arguments about chocolate chips and whether eating too much coconut gave you diarrhea.

He was tired of having seven identical suits and a humidity controlled wardrobe and a nice apartment and a nice car and still being alone all the time.

He was tired because he had met someone and watched her leave and done nothing about it. He should have called her, but he didn't know what to say.

Daniel Bearing was tired of it all. He needed a holiday. He went to see his father. He had nowhere else to go.

date night again

It was called 'Hanging Out.' It was a gallery opening and a singles night all rolled into one. It sounded like a terrible idea. It was. Matt knew it the moment he walked through the door. It was even worse than he had imagined.

The gallery was all bare brick and exposed pipes and shiny vinyl flooring with half a dozen vast canvases each trapped in their own pool of acid light. That wasn't the worst part. The canvases were all blue. They were new work by Jack Eastleigh. Matt's ex brother-in-law.

Matt was about to turn around and leave when he saw a familiar face in the sparse crowd. It was the woman with the red hair and freckles that he had met a few weeks earlier. Even staring at a blue canvas she looked like trouble.

'Charlotte?' Matt said, closing the distance between them with a couple of strides, a sideways shimmy and a well-placed elbow.

'Hey. The sofa guy,' Charlotte said.

'Matt,' Matt said, just in case she had forgotten his name.

'I remember. Long time no see. You didn't come back.'

'It wasn't really my sort of thing,' Matt said.

'So you thought you'd give this a try instead?' She said doubtfully.

'I didn't think you'd be here.'

Charlotte frowned. 'Thanks.'

Matt looked hurt. 'I didn't mean it like that.'

Charlotte laughed. 'I know,' she said. 'I'm just messing with you. How's the divorce going?'

'I think I've got the sofa,' Matt said.

'Good for you. Must be a fantastic piece of furniture.'

'No. It isn't. Not really.'

Matt could feel elevator doors slowly opening in his heart. That's what it felt like. They slid apart silently. There was no elevator waiting beyond them. Just a deep shaft of meaningless nothing. Matt felt a sickening lurch as he stepped into the void.

'So, what do you do Matt?' Charlotte said.

'I'm not sure anymore,' Matt said.

'Interesting answer,' Charlotte said, moving towards the next blue canvas, even though it was practically identical to the one she had just been looking at.

'I'm still sorting a few things out. Back in my old room at mum's. Haven't even unpacked. Living out of bin liners. Can't seem to get my head straight.' Matt stopped himself going any further. 'Sorry,' he said. 'I can't believe I just told you that.'

'Don't apologise,' Charlotte said. 'You were just being honest. I haven't heard honesty in a while. Most of the people here tonight won't even write their real name on a sticky label. Half the men are married. Some of the women too. Everyone's lying about something. Pick anyone in the room and I bet they're ten years older than they say they are.'

'Do you want me to go away?' Matt said.

'No,' she said. 'How about we start over?'

'Really?'

'Yeah. Why not? From the beginning.'

'I'd like that.'

'Okay.'

Matt took a deep breath, He shook out his hands. He loosened his shoulders. He was about to reach down and touch his toes when Charlotte gave him one of those 'get on with it' looks. He stuck his hand out towards her.

'Hi Charlotte,' he said. 'My name's Matt. Matthew. I'm twenty-nine and I don't have a clue what I'm doing here.'

Charlotte looked amused and then suspicious.

'Would I lie to you?' Matt added.

'I figured you more for a Colin or a Neil,' Charlotte said. 'And maybe late thirties or early forties.'

'Thanks,' Matt said. 'Sorry to disappoint you.'

'Did I say I was disappointed?' Charlotte said.

A moment happened between them. A spark of something. A crackle.

'Can I get you a drink?' Matt said.

'No thanks,' Charlotte said. 'I was just leaving. Nice to meet you Matt. My name's Grace.'

5 things about Grace

Grace was trouble. Not in a bad way. She had attitude. It was hard to miss. She had short red hair and freckles and a great voice that was gutsy and soulful, and she sang in a band and worked in a comic shop and had her bicycle stolen all the time because she never chained it up properly. Grace treated bicycles like wild birds and refused to keep them in a cage.

Grace was confident and fearless, but her heart was understandably wary.

Grace was unexpectedly single. It was a shock and a relief and a betrayal and lots of other things that she couldn't put a name too. Mostly she found it funny. For months she couldn't take love seriously at all.

Grace didn't want to be single forever. It was a difficult transition. The letters were a constant reminder of the absurdity of it all.

Grace received 7 letters in total. They were all from Andy. He was an ex-boyfriend. The one before Greg. They were written on lined paper and folded into tight bundles that sat uncomfortably in an envelope. Grace didn't answer any of them.

7 letters to Grace

Dear Grace

Don't marry Greg. Greg is an idiot. He will never make you happy like I could. I know I screwed up and I don't deserve a second chance. Technically a third chance. I know I screwed up the second chance. I was mixed up and immature and I didn't mean it. None of it. It was all a mistake. Both times. Just don't marry Greg. Greg is an idiot. I don't know what else to say. Call me sometime.

Andy x

Dear Grace

I have just heard that you aren't marrying Greg anymore. Michelle told me. I am truly sorry to hear that. I hope it was nothing I said? Greg is an idiot, but he is my best friend, so I can say that about him.

I have been seeing Michelle off and on but it's nothing serious. I like her though. She wants to get married, but I don't want to. Call me when you get this and we can have a drink and talk about giving me another chance. Don't tell Michelle about this letter if you see her. Or the other

one. She doesn't know that it is on and off between us. We
see things differently. She thinks it is mostly on with only
the occasional off. I see our relationship as mostly off with
the occasional on. I don't want to mess up what we've got
if you decide not to give me another chance after all. That
would ruin everything. Thanks for not telling her. Call me.

Andy x

Dear Grace

I have spoken to Greg and he says he has no idea why
you called the wedding off. I can't believe you did that to
him. He's a nice guy. He's an idiot, but he's also my best
friend, so I can say that about him. He is furious. I don't
know what to say. At least I had nothing to do with you
splitting up. Or did I? I'm mixed up. Call me and we can
have a drink and maybe a nice meal and talk about giving
me another chance now that Greg has decided that he
doesn't want you back. I don't blame him. Call me.

Andy x

Dear Grace

Sorry about my last letter. It was a mistake. I got my
wires crossed. I didn't have all the facts, and for that I
apologise. Michelle has met Greg's new girlfriend, and she
is pregnant. Very. That is why you called off the wedding.
I can see that now. Greg is an idiot. He's my best friend
and everything, but sometimes he makes me so mad I could
shout at him. Greg wants to know if he can have the
engagement ring back. He would ask you himself, but he's

scared to. He's an idiot. I haven't met his girlfriend yet, but Michelle says she is very nice and isn't like you at all. Is that supposed to mean something? We had some good times together. I know I screwed up, but I'm over that now. Call me.

Andy x

Dear Grace
Greg asked me to say thank you for returning his engagement ring. He's an idiot. If you have nothing to do next Thursday, I am available. Michelle is going out with Rachel and Paige, so I won't have to tell her where I am going. I'm serious. Call me.

Andy x

Dear Grace
How are you? I am fine. You didn't call me, so Michelle and I are getting married. Isn't that great news? Sarah-Jane didn't want the engagement ring that you gave back to Greg, so I gave it to Michelle instead. Hope you don't mind? I didn't tell her where I got it from. Michelle says you aren't seeing anyone at the moment. You almost did, but you changed your mind when you found out he wasn't really divorced yet. What a creep.

Call me when you get this and maybe I will change my mind about the whole wedding thing. We have a lot to talk about.

Andy x

The Map of Us

Dear Grace

*I am sorry that you were not able to come to our wedding
because you were not invited for technical reasons. It rained.
The band were dreadful and so was the cake. I'm married
now, so I think I should stop writing to you – unless you
want me to?*

Call me if you do.

Andy x

E

Abby was sitting in the back of a car. She had a seatbelt on. She had her school bag beside her on the seat. She had a box of orange juice with a straw. It was warm. She drank it anyway.

Abby did not know where she was going. She looked out of the window but outside meant nothing to her. She did not know where it was, and it was going by too fast. It was getting dark.

Abby didn't go in cars that much. Francesca Drinkwater's mum had a car. She had gone home in that car once. It was full of crisps and dropped sweets and seats for babies. Francesca had two brothers and a sister. They were all babies. Abby didn't have a brother or a sister. Just a mum. Abby's mum didn't have a car. It was easier for her.

'I'm Mrs Haddon,' the lady driving said.

Abby didn't say anything.

'I'm a social worker,' the lady said.

Abby didn't know what that was.

'Do you know what that means?' the lady said.

Abby nodded even though she didn't. She had almost finished her juice.

'Do you have anyone we can call?' the lady said.

Abby wanted to go home. And another juice. She looked out of the window and watched the world she knew turn into a blur.

37 words

It was late afternoon. Sometime in June. Violet could not be certain whereabouts in June, for it had not occurred to her to make a record. She did not dance to the music of time. She had a slower step.

She had just passed the remains of a frost-shattered milestone on her left and was uncertain which direction to take at the crossroads still some considerable distance ahead. Whether to skirt around the enclosures and cross the stream at the first opportunity, or crest the hill and take the longer route across the common. All in her mind at least. Her thoughts had been interrupted at a critical moment. There was a man at the door.

At first Violet thought it might be another unwanted visitor looking for the home of Arthur Galbraith. She peered through the curtains in the front parlour. The man standing on the doorstep did not look like the others who had arrived unannounced. He had a spade. And a dog.

She opened the door. Only a little. The man ran a muddy hand through his hair and stood up straight. The dog sat down. The two things happened simultaneously. Violet smiled unintentionally. She was hoping to be stern and dismissive.

'Yes?' she said.

'You have a large garden,' he said.

'Yes,' she said.

'I am a gardener,' he said.

She nodded. She had no knowledge of whether he was a gardener or not, but it was statement said with such complete confidence that she felt obliged to reward it in some way.

'Looking for work,' he added.

'Indeed,' she said.

'Would there be any work in your garden?'

'Yes,' Violet said, for she knew there was.

'Good,' he said.

'Good,' she said.

'Shall I come back tomorrow then and make a start?'

'Yes,' she said – and closed the door.

That was the sum total of their conversation. It lasted less than a minute, contained 37 words, an unintentional smile and a rewarding nod – and was about to change the direction of two lives forever. Three if you count the dog.

sandwich

Shortly after dawn, he arrived. Violet did not hear for she slept soundly – dreaming of adventures that would not be hers but another's.

He brought with him a wheelbarrow and tools and an old hat and a dog and a sandwich wrapped in a sheet of newspaper. It was not so much a sandwich as a loaf of bread, still warm to the touch, the centre scooped out and replaced with a wedge of strong cheese. A sandwich fit for a gardener.

The dog would normally ride in the barrow. It was easier that way. He was the king of dogs with his own carriage. His ears were up. He had never been to this garden before. There was no telling what might happen. Perhaps a rat or a slowworm or a shady patch or an intriguing smell or an annoying fly or a tail to chase in endless stupid circles or some other amusement befitting a dog that arrived in a carriage.

And later, perhaps, a piece of sandwich that was not quite a sandwich in the truest sense, but a sandwich that knew its place in things and wore a coat that rustled so that its unwrapping could be easily heard by a dog.

It was a good day, started early and finished late and full of the precious gift of small wonders.

The gardener and his dog and their sandwich set about their work.

roses

Violet awoke to find things much changed. The view from her room had shifted. A small area of the garden had been tamed. A fire had been started. A wheelbarrow was piled high with dry poppy heads and weeds. An old hat was perched on a low wall next to an object wrapped in newspaper. There were snails on both. Hundreds of them covered the wall. They had been evicted from their homes. They were scattering in all directions, both vertical and horizontal. Some were bright yellow. Others had stripes of brown and black. They had a long journey ahead of them.

Violet could see the dog but not the gardener. The dog could see her too. She got dressed as quickly as she was able. It was not usually a process she enjoyed, but today was different. Today there was something outside the house she was eager to be a part of.

The key in the back door turned but was not happy about it. The door opened, tearing away the knitting of a decade of spiders. And Violet felt the sun on her face. She was not sure at first whether she liked it. She looked down.

There on the step was an old bottle only recently pulled

from the ground. She could see where he had tried to clean it off. The trail of his fingers across the muddy glass. In it were two perfect roses. One was a deep orange. The other would be the colour of red wine. She could not be sure. Violet had only ever seen wine in pictures.

She picked up the bottle. The roses were scented. She smiled, as she would do many times from now on. The bottle changed in her hand. It was cut glass. Tall and thin. She took the flowers to her study. The back door she left open.

royalty

The dog looked at the sandwich that was not a sandwich with an intensity that could melt lead. The gardener had stopped for a while and found an apple tree to lean against and was reading the sheet of newspaper that wrapped the sandwich even though it was more than a year old. He read with a finger that followed the words. Sometimes it retraced its steps to make better sense of what was written.

The dog looked at the sandwich.

The fire was burning hot now and had lost its swirling hair of smoke. The wheelbarrow had been emptied. There was much to burn. The garden was large.

Violet watched him from her study window. She could not write. Not yet. No one had given her flowers before. Roses or otherwise. She was twenty-eight years old and she did not know what it meant. She was curious and surprised and cautious and felt suddenly alive.

The gardener was called Owen. He did not have another name. Not one that he could be certain of. It was lost somewhere on the way to here, and it was too late for him to turn back and search for it. It no longer mattered. It was like a story in a year-old newspaper that no one cared about. Not anymore.

The dog looked at the sandwich.

The dog was called Dog. It was enough. He was brown and white and big enough to ride in a wheelbarrow.

Owen tore off a piece of bread and threw it in the air. The dog watched as it somersaulted and tumbled. He was a king. He had his own carriage. He would wait until it was dignified to eat it. It landed on the ground in front of him. Then it was gone.

28 minutes

It started promptly at 10.37am on the morning of April 22nd and was all over by 11.05am on the same day. Practically. By 11.12am I had a fair idea where my bra was and had sight of at least one shoe. It took until 11.18am to find the other one. It was hiding under the bed. I had no recollection of taking it off. Or my bra. Or the rest of my clothes. Or the long over-coat with a zip and buttons that usually takes me half an hour to escape. Everything happened so promptly, I rather got carried away with the moment. I must have undressed at record speed.

There was a large clock on the wall. It had a dark wooden case and Roman numerals instead of numbers and had a reassuringly calm tick. It was about the only thing in the room that remained reassuringly calm. I don't know why I kept one eye on the time. I have thought about it often since. Somehow I thought it might be important. It wasn't. I don't know why I didn't have my eyes closed or something. I usually do. Mostly anyway. Sometimes I like to watch. But I've never timed it before. Never. Not accurately. I'm not sure that the pillow case was clean either.

It was okay. Okay for twenty-eight minutes. Practically. I suppose. I wasn't thinking about the consequences then. I was focused on getting my clothes back on. The consequences would come later. Not as much later as I had hoped. By 11.27am I was walking down the corridor towards the hotel reception for the second time.

It was a Thursday. It was raining outside. That sort of fine rain that seems like it's going to build-up to something and then never does. I'm not sure if that is relevant or not. 10.37am and the rain outside seemed to have something in common.

Twenty-eight minutes. Let's call it half an hour for the sake of argument. I'm not even sure that qualifies as an affair. I've done some research and can't find any firm criteria. It wasn't a one-night stand. That much is fairly obvious. It happened in the morning. For less than half an hour. I knew what I was doing. Or at least I thought I did at the time.

I have regrets. Of course I do. It was stupid. I wish now that we had closed the curtains.

finished

When the first draft of my report was finished, it contained three Venn diagrams, a histogram, five pie-charts, a line graph and a colour-coded flow chart snappily entitled '10.37am – Twenty-Eight Minutes of My Life That Were Okay, I Suppose.' I probably should have shortened it a little, but in some ways I thought it was already short enough.

The Compatibility Index contained one hundred and twenty questions in twelve separate sections. Section Twelve was not perhaps as well defined as it might have been. It was where I put all the miscellaneous questions that I liked the sound of but couldn't find a place for anywhere else. In the end I decided to call it 'Section 12: Miscellaneous Questions' for that reason.

I did try and find another name that wasn't quite so blindingly obvious. 'Assorted Questions' made it sound like a box of broken biscuits. 'Motley Questions' lacked charm. 'Indiscriminate Questions' was too close to the truth for comfort. Then I gave up for a while. Half a bar of chocolate later I decided that boring and obvious was perfectly acceptable, and I really did have other more important things to be getting on with – like eating the rest of the chocolate.

All that remained was to print the Compatibility Index and the scoring sheets that went with it. I chose to do that at work. Yeah. You guessed it. That was a mistake.

calibrating

The printer at work is a grey plastic tower block with strange-looking balconies and multiple paper trays and a complicated control panel and a small display screen and lots of little numbered buttons and one big green button that says 'Okay' for no apparent reason. You only press it when things are not okay and you're trying to stop it doing something it shouldn't. Pressing the 'Okay' button doesn't actually stop it doing something it shouldn't. I guess it's just there to make you feel better about wasting half a ream of paper printing something you didn't want to.

The printer is directly outside my office door. I can see it through the glass partition. It used to be outside Helen's office, right next to a spare power socket. She didn't like it being there. She was a bridesmaid at Trish's wedding, so it was moved. Now it sits outside my office with a long extension lead stuck to the floor tiles with about a mile of grey duct tape. It's an obvious trip hazard, but Helen was a bridesmaid at Trish's wedding, so we all just had to learn to live with it.

I pressed 'Print' on my laptop.

Nothing happened.

Then something happened.

Then it stopped happening.

Then some lights flashed on the control panel.

A red exclamation mark blinked.

Then that went out.

Then I went to see what was going on.

Then the red light came back on again, this time with a green light that said 'Ready.'

Then it all went quiet again.

Then I pressed the 'Okay' button...

...and nothing happened.

The display screen said 'Please Wait. Printing Document.'

But it wasn't.

Then it said 'Cleaning.'

Then it said 'Warming Up.'

Then it said 'Please Wait' again.

Then I pressed the 'Okay' button about six times.

Noting happened.

Then the printer said 'Low on Toner.'

It wasn't.

Then it said 'Paper Tray 2 is Empty.'

It wasn't.

Then it stopped saying anything for a while and made a series of rumbling and whirring noises that slowly built to a crescendo and then ended with a highly satisfying 'clunk.' It reminded me of one of Matt's jazz records.

Then the printer said it was 'Calibrating.'

In my experience, 'Calibrating' meant that the printer was broken indefinitely. Like a month-old washing machine with soapy water pouring through a split in the door seal.

I wondered where my brother had got to.

brushstrokes

Kiss.

'Next is a Vigo Gualdrini portrait of Theonistus of Milan. 1490. Robe. Less than two inches. Should take me about a year. Maybe 18 months depending on the condition of the underlying painting,' Nadia said.

Kiss.

'Then I've got a Federigo Badoer portrait of an unknown merchant. 1521. Robe. Hairline crack. At least two years.'

Long kiss.

'Then a Cento Ferrazzetta altarpiece. 1504. A year. Followed by a triptych on oak panels that was damaged in an earthquake. Baptista Majoli. 1489. I've only seen photographs. It's in a bad way. Probably a decade.'

Kiss

'Then a really big job. *"The Battle of Cremona de Santa"* by Luca Battista Bussi. 1463. Large piece. Fifteen years.'

Half a kiss. An interrupted kiss. A kiss that that was broken by surprise.

'You have the rest of your life mapped out already?' Jack said.

'Yes,' Nadia said with little enthusiasm. 'I seem to paint my life one tiny brushstroke at a time. With a month off in between. Don't stop kissing.'

'I won't,' Jack said.

Kiss.

'I'm glad,' Nadia said.

late

Jack finally turned up at the offices of Compass Applied Analytics five days later than planned. Trish kept him waiting in reception while she checked his credentials, and Helen looked out of her office window to see if there were any skateboards left outside in the car park. No one offered him a coffee. Even when I told them who he was I wasn't sure they believed me.

'This is Jack Eastleigh,' I said.

'Really?' Trish said, wasp firmly in-ear.

'He doesn't look like a world authority on the colour blue,' Helen whispered, loud enough so that we could all hear. So not really whispered at all. Just in a low husky voice.

'It's okay. It happens all the time,' Jack said. Like he always says. He smiled too. Jack has a great smile. Even for someone who doesn't look like he should.

Helen melted. Her shoulders sagged, and her head flopped to one side. For a moment, even Trish's wasp seemed to have found a way out of her ear – before doing a quick loop of the reception area and flying straight back in again.

'You're five days late,' Trish said. And then Jack was bustled off into the conference room to discuss blackcurrant and blueberry smoothies.

promises

Matt's mother called later. She wanted her wedding gift back. She couldn't remember what it was. She thought that it could have been a pair of candlesticks or some champagne flutes or a small silver picture frame. It wasn't. She didn't actually give us anything, I remember. All we got from her was an envelope with a note inside. It was an IOU of sorts. It was written on the back of a shopping list. She promised to give us some money towards the honeymoon, but it never materialised.

The envelope had her address crossed out on the front and the stamp torn off. It was folded in half, and the edges were crumpled. It's probably in the drawer underneath the coffee table in the hallway. She can have the envelope back if I find it.

5 things about
Matt's mother

Matt's mother turned up to our wedding wearing a hat made of feathers that looked like a parrot had crashed into the side of her head. She wanted to be the centre of attention. She was. She drank. She fell over. She danced. She fell over again. She started to sing. We called her a taxi and sent her home. I paid for it.

Matt's mother has always been rude to me. Right from the start. She began with condescending and scornful. Then she slowly worked her way up to tactless, insulting and perfunctory. I thought things were improving between us when she introduced mocking and contemptuous to her extensive repertoire. I was mistaken. Now that she has a real reason to be rude to me she doesn't know what to say. She's lost. She peaked too soon. Her impoliteness has nowhere else to go.

Matt's mother wanted to come and live with us while she was having double glazing installed. Matt said 'yes' without asking me. When I came home and found her sitting on the sofa drinking a bottle of my 'special occasion' wine I called her a taxi and sent her home. It took two. One for her and one for all her luggage. Matt said that I was being selfish and cruel. I thought he was overreacting. She was only having a new front door fitted. I paid for the taxi. Both of them. And the wine. I was looking forward to that.

Matt's mother has special dietary requirements that seem to vary depending on which celebrity fad diet she has just finished reading about in a magazine. At the wedding she demanded that everything was organic, vegan and gluten-free. Even the cake. The cake looked like a soggy mattress with blueberries carelessly scattered on top. It *tasted* like a soggy mattress with blueberries carelessly scattered on top. Matt's mother didn't have to eat it. She was being sick in the back of a taxi on her way home by then. I had to pay to clean that up, too.

Matt's mother has been married six times. Hard to believe. I've met her. Four of her six ex-husbands had to be invited to our wedding. It made the table plan a little tricky. She is currently on the lookout for husband number seven. 'Prowling' is a word that I rarely get to use. In her case it seems appropriate.

hard to tell

Matt called a few days later.

'Mum wants to know why you haven't returned her wedding present yet,' he said.

'What was it? I said.

'I don't know,' he said.

'I don't know either,' I said. I did, but as she had given us a secondhand envelope containing a worthless note written on the back of a shopping list I felt that I was well within my rights to plead ignorance.

'So, are you going to send it back or what?' He said.

'How can I if I don't know what it was?' I said.

'Well, send her some money then,' he said.

'Why?'

'Because she bought us something and she wants it back,' he said, beginning to lose his temper.

Anything involving his mother always made Matt lose his temper. She had the same effect on me.

'No,' I said.

I don't know who hung up first. I think it was me, but it's hard to tell. I'd hung up.

144

impulsive

I don't know if all the hanging up was what made me do it. Maybe it *was* all the hanging up? Maybe it was getting on my nerves. I'd like to think that I wasn't just being spiteful. Maybe I *was* just being spiteful? It all happened so quickly. A bit like 10.37am. I'm not normally so impulsive. Maybe I *am* impulsive? Maybe I've been underestimating my capacity for impulsiveness all these years? Maybe that was what it was? I'm not sure that two impulsive acts made me an impulsive person. A bit like I wasn't sure whether 10.37am qualified as an actual affair or not.

Whatever. I did it. I sent Matt a copy of the preliminary report.

Not the Compatibility Index and the score sheets, but everything else. The summary and the diagrams and the footnotes and conclusions. I put it all in a big brown envelope and sent it to his mother's house.

The moment I folded and crushed and jammed and cajoled the envelope into a postbox, I knew there would be a lot more hanging up in the future.

I was wrong.

top bunk

Matt was in his old bedroom at his mum's house. It had spaceship wallpaper and curtains with footballs on them. He had bunk beds even though there was only him. He was sleeping on the top bunk. He never used to sleep on the top bunk, but this was different. He was grown up now and didn't want to be reminded of the smaller version of himself that slept on the bottom bunk and peeled the wallpaper and drilled holes in the plaster with a pen top and had to remember what to call his new step dad every five minutes.

He could hear his mother singing downstairs. He had no idea what she was singing about. She had the voice of a squashed angel.

Matt hated being back where he started. He hated not having somewhere to take Grace. He hated the stupid bunk beds and the wallpaper and the curtains and the sense that he was shrinking and becoming a child again. Above all he hated the sound of his mother singing. Singing was a sign. Singing meant that she had found someone new. Singing meant that she was planning on saying 'Yes' and getting married again and that there would soon be a new name to memorise and call dad – but only if he wanted to.

The doorbell rang. His mother stopped singing. That was good. It was the postman. That wasn't.

where Matt was

Matt was not exactly lost. No. To be lost you have to leave somewhere and not be able to find your way to somewhere else. Matt knew where he was, he just wasn't sure what he was doing there. He wasn't at a crossroads or a junction or a fork in the road. He never made it that far.

Matt had no clear direction to speak of. He was a paper bag somersaulting down a January street to the sound of a dog barking, that's all.

Matt was waiting for something to happen. It was hard to tell what. He didn't know. He liked to think about his future while he was asleep on a secondhand sofa. For all he knew his future may have already come and gone. Like a golden sofa of infinite possibilities gliding serenely past while he slept.

spoilage

Dog watching me.
Go away dog.
Know what you're thinking.
Beard.
Eyebrows.
Sitting.
Watching.
Tail wagging.
Mad eyes.
Bit of collie.
Short legs.
Spaniel.
Bit of something else.
Something.
Wiry.
Mostly grey.
Go away dog.
Concentrate.
Undercut.
Shape.

Brush.
Better.
Look up.
Dog watching.
Yard closer maybe.
Hard to tell.
Sitting.
Mad eyes.
Know that look.
Know what it's thinking.
Go away dog.
Concentrate.
Undercut.
Shape.
Brush.
Again.
Undercut.
Shape.
Brush.
Bloody apples.
Better.
Look up.
Dog watching.
Yard closer.
A familiar sense of looming dread.
Second Place.
Lose points for 'spoilage.'
That's what they call it.

'Spoilage: The unforeseen erosion of detail in the period between sculpting and judging.'
Idiot.
What was I thinking?
Sand sculpture of a tree.
An apple tree.
Any tree.
On a beach.
Miles from a tree.
Any tree.
Idiot.
Go away dog.

a 'friend'

I finally called Bearing Foods. I'd been putting it off. I didn't want to talk to Daniel Bearing about 'Seedy-Pea-Nut-Slices.' I didn't want to talk to him at all. I'd only met him briefly. It seemed like a long time ago. It wasn't that long. It seemed like it. So much had happened in between.

I didn't want to call Daniel Bearing, but I didn't have a choice. I didn't want to get called to Trish's office again and be told off by someone wearing stripes with a wasp in her ear. I already had a headache.

I sighed. I looked out of the window. I rearranged some coloured pencils on my desk. I thought about getting some water. I already had some. I frowned. I sighed again. I dialed the number.

He was out of the office. His secretary said he was on holiday. She did not know when he would be back. She asked who was calling and I said 'a friend.' I don't know why I said that. She asked if I'd like to leave a message, but I said that it was okay and didn't leave one.

I put the phone down and held my head in my hands. It was so embarrassing.

in-flight

Daniel Bearing flew from London to Inverness and then boarded a connecting flight on to Stornoway. He read the in-flight magazine and worked out all the other places he could have flown to in the same time if he wasn't so tired.

The plane was small and had propellers and rattled and seemed to be made of plastic panels that didn't quite fit together. There was a Bearing Foods snack bar wrapper pushed into gaping hole behind the armrest. 'Apricot & Carrot Oat Crumble.' It was one of the older recipes but still sold well. It was getting expensive to produce though. Margins were tight. The price of dried apricots had been rising steadily. Increasing the proportion of oats had helped to absorb some of the extra cost, but adding more carrot made the product taste soapy and unappealing. A decision to reduce the size of the bar was overdue.

Daniel tried to sleep, but the flight only lasted 45 minutes. He had barely got comfortable and they were landing.

south and a little west

Daniel Bearing hired a car at Stornoway airport.

He didn't need directions. There was only one road. He was told to follow the road south and then a little west. When the road ran into the ocean he would be where he was going. Daniel found such simplicity hard to believe. He got in the car and drove south and then a little west. Sure enough, when he reached the ocean, he was at his father's house.

strangers

Katherine was standing alone in her handbag room staring at her collection of polka dot totes. She had four of them. They had all been perfect in their time. When she bought them. The receipts were inside. She could check. She didn't want to look. She didn't want to be reminded. She felt empty. She didn't know what to do with the feeling. What could you do to fill such emptiness? She had tried. She had over three hundred handbags laid out on glass shelves in their own room, and it made no difference.

The room was white. Like all the other rooms in the modern and minimalist house she shared with her husband. The lighting was subtle and infinitely adjustable. She adjusted it. She had a small remote control. It was easily lost. It was white. She changed the colour and brightness. But nothing looked right. She changed it again. It was all ugly and broken. The handbags meant nothing to her. She felt no attachment to any of them. They were strangers to her. Days like this were happening more often than she dared to admit.

She left the room and locked the door. There was no reason to lock the door. Clive would not go inside. He had never been inside. He did not want to go inside. That was part of the problem. That was his part of the problem anyway.

She was losing him.

SE

Abby was in another office. It had seven desks in it. It looked like a classroom. There were computers and folders and plastic trays and chairs with wheels. Abby wasn't sitting on a chair with wheels. She had been sitting on a chair with wheels, but Mrs Haddon had told her to stop. Now she was on a chair without wheels. It was soft though. Not like school chairs.

'We're trying to locate your family,' Mrs Haddon said. Abby couldn't help with that. She didn't have any. Just her mum. Her mum said it was easier that way.

Mrs Haddon started looking through Abby's schoolbag. She didn't ask first. There was a pencil and a ruler and a book. The book was not a school book. It was a copy of *Galbraith's Boot* Volume 7: 'Walks From Claystones to Meddle-on-the-Moor.'

Mrs Haddon opened the front cover. There was something written inside. 'Property of David North' it said. It was almost scratched through the paper.

Mrs Haddon showed Abby the book.

'Who gave you this?' she said.

'Granddad,' Abby said.

Granddad told her it was written by a witch. But it was a good book. She liked it. It had pictures.

path

Arthur Galbraith would go no further. He refused. He sat on a rock by the side of a pool of clear water and held his head in his hands. He had been there for three days now. Violet could find no way of persuading him to move on. The road ahead was obvious. He did not seem to care. The weather was agreeable for the season. It did not matter to him if it rained or snowed. She pleaded and urged. He would not listen.

Violet was losing patience. The route up through the hollows had been steep but unremarkable. There was a wide valley with a fine granite circle almost in sight. She had placed few real obstacles in his way, yet he had been surly and unco-operative for much of the current volume.

She left him there for another day. It would not hurt him to be alone and think about his behaviour. She placed a cloth over her typewriter and went out into the garden. A path was beginning to appear. A way forward through the tangle of brambles and cow parsley. Owen was in the distance, in some part of the dense undergrowth that had not yet surrendered to the sharp edge of a billhook. He stopped and glanced back

159

at her. She was brave. She held his glance for a moment more than was perhaps appropriate.

At last she had guessed at her fictional hero's trouble.

Arthur Galbraith was sulking.

He was jealous.

closer

At last, Volume 3: 'Walks from Bishop's Top to Nine Ways End' was complete. It had taken some time longer than expected. Violet found Owen a constant distraction.

Every morning there would be fresh flowers waiting for her by the back door. She could hear him working in the garden. Sometimes distant. Sometimes outside her study window. It made no difference which. It was a large garden, but she knew that he was always close by.

Violet kept a tall pile of sketches on her desk. They were unlabeled. She chose a selection from the bottom of the pile and randomly incorporated them into the text. They were all much the same. All hills and valleys and clouds and rivers. Or rivers and valleys and clouds and hills. She would draw them two dozen at a time with a dip pen and a bottle of Indian ink. She found the bottle in her brother's room on the third floor of the house.

It took her an hour to climb the stairs. She knew that David had a pen and ink. He liked to stab at her with the nib or flick ink at her and then run away laughing. There were other things inside his room that she remembered, too. There were broken stair spindles. Some of them had been sharpened. And two heavy dictionaries, bound in red leather with gold embossed lettering. She remembered those well. She took what she needed and did not go to his room again.

Violet wrapped the completed manuscript in brown paper and addressed it to her publisher. Owen would take it to the village when he was finished for the day. She would hand it to him in person. Perhaps their hands might touch, if only for a moment. It would be the closest they had ever been.

closer still

Owen had nothing to give her apart from flowers from her own garden. The time for flowers would soon be at an end. What then? He could not leave bare sticks in a jar. It worried him.

He left flowers to please her. He watched her take them inside. He watched her place them on the desk next to her typewriter. They would be her companion while she worked. They were her flowers. She would not come outside. She was scared to leave the house. She was beautiful and did not know it. No one had ever spoken to her of love.

Owen had a wheelbarrow and a spade and a dog and little talent for words. He spoke to the garden because it was polite to ask first. He must sometimes be cruel, and he did not want the garden to think that it was without purpose. He explained. The garden was large. He had much to say.

He agreed to take a parcel to the village for her. It was wrapped in brown paper. It was a book. Her book. He made sure his hands were clean. Nothing could be done about the state of his fingernails. He was a gardener. It was a little earth he would carry with him always. She handed him the package. Their hands touched, if only for a moment.

Jules Preston

Owen knew then, as he had always known. There would be no bare sticks in a jar. She would always have flowers. He would speak to the garden. He would mend the greenhouse. He would do anything.

gift

Owen cut back the honeysuckle and wisteria and clematis and ivy and found a peach tree trained against the south-facing wall. There was a single peach. Not yet ripe. There was a pear tree too, but no pears to be seen.

Owen cut the grass and found the shape of lawns beneath. And gravel paths that led away from the house. He would clear them when he had more time.

He dug flower beds and made hedges look like castle battlements.

Owen drove the wasps from the apple tree with fire and smoke and damp grass cuttings and a gentle east wind. They would not return.

He pulled ivy from the upper windows of the house – though there was no one to look out of them. He made certain that the windows opened and the frames were still sound.

He cleared and repainted the wrought iron fence. He found new slates for the roof of the potting shed and glass for the greenhouse. He built new shelves inside.

Jules Preston

The garden began to believe in itself again.

When he had finished, the peach was ripe. He gave it to Violet.

doors

The next morning Violet found flowers waiting for her outside the back door as usual – they were pink rose mallow – and beside them was a peach.

It was such an unexpected gift that she laughed out loud. Owen heard her. He could ask for no more.

Violet took the flowers inside and put them next to her typewriter as she always did. Then she went back to the kitchen and found a knife and a plate and cut the peach in two. She removed the stone and set it aside to dry on the windowsill. She would keep it. It would be placed on her desk next to the typewriter and remain there forever as a reminder that great treasures come in all sizes and appear in odd ways.

She took the plate to the back door. It was not easy for her to walk and carry the plate at the same time, but she would try. Now was no time to be concerned by the tyranny of doors and what lay beyond them.

She could see a path ahead. It was gravel. She remembered it. She remembered the sound of the stones as they pushed her wheelchair out into the sun when she was younger. Waiting for the sound of their footsteps to return as it got dark. Realising that they would not come. Making herself as warm as she could. Listening to other sounds through long hours. Hoping for the moon to break through the clouds.

She would not be stopped. She went out into the garden.

tablecloth

Owen could hear her coming. He would not go to help. She would not want that. That was not the part he played in all of this. He had time to prepare.

He upturned a bucket. It would be a low table. He unwrapped his sandwich that was not a sandwich and used the sheet of newspaper as a tablecloth. It was not fine lace, but it would do. He folded the edges over. That would do better.

There was a cast iron bench that he had recently found buried in brambles. It was not far off. He dragged it to the table. He still had time. The bench was rusty. He sat on it where she might sit. It was not so rusty afterwards. It was the best that he could do.

Then she appeared. She was carrying a plate. On the plate were two halves of the peach that he had given her. She found a table and a tablecloth and a bench that was not as rusty as it might have been.

She had come further than she thought was possible. She no longer feared the garden. There was something in it that was worth walking for.

The dog did not notice. He looked at the unwrapped sandwich with fierce concentration.

true

It was December. Six months had passed since Owen had arrived at her doorstep. The dog was waiting in the wheelbarrow that was a carriage for a king. The day was at an end. He was leaving. Violet had come to hate these moments. He stood at the back door as he always did. Every day since sometime in June. He would not go until he had said goodbye.

'You are finished then?' Violet asked.

'There is nothing more for me to do.'

'Yes,' she said.

'Winter is here.'

'Yes,' she said.

'The garden needs to sleep. I must not be here to wake it.'

She knew it was true. He had stayed too long already.

'You will return in the Spring? she asked.

'Perhaps,' he said.

She did not know what he meant by that.

'There is something else?' Violet asked, telling herself not to hope.

'There is,' he said.

He ran a muddy hand through his hair as he done the first

day they met, when he had turned up unannounced on her doorstep and she had tried to be stern and dismissive and found herself smiling despite herself. She had done the same so many times since.

'I never want to leave your side,' he said.

It was statement and a question and a plea and a proposal and a warm breath on a cold day and a desperate heartbeat.

'Yes,' she said.

And that was enough.

True to his word, he never did.

172

output

There was a note on my desk. It was a message from the Marketing Executive at Bearing Foods. The company were discontinuing the 'Seedy-Pea-Nut Slice' development program. They were focusing instead on snack bars with a higher coconut content and products that contained chocolate chips. Daniel Bearing was still on holiday. I wondered what he thought of the changes.

The printer had stopped calibrating, but there was no sign of my printouts. There were several other documents piled in the output tray. Some were over a week old.

There was a quote for a set of skeleton keys and lock picks that I assumed belonged to Helen.

There were pictures of an ankle length, vertical stripe, belted shirt dress and a pair of strappy black platforms with a five-inch heel that that were definitely Trish's.

There was no Compatibility Index or copies of the score sheets. They would turn up eventually.

I had a few of the earlier versions at home. I could use those for now.

68%

I completed our Compatibility Index in about an hour. I tried to be as objective as I could. I calculated that any error caused by personal bias was no greater than plus or minus 3%. I had no real evidence to suggest that this degree of accuracy was correct, but it sounded about right. There was no point getting hung up about it. I had a bottle of wine and a large glass, and that seemed to help.

It took me a further quarter of an hour to add up the results on the score sheet. Then, because I had a bottle of wine and a large glass, I added them up again to make sure I hadn't made a mistake somewhere. I hadn't.

I couldn't believe it. We scored a solid 68%. On the surface, it appeared that Matt and I were perfect for each other. Why hadn't I noticed before? Why didn't it feel that way? Then I remembered that I was dealing with statistics and they always told two stories.

We were 68% compatible, which meant that we were also 32% incompatible. Almost a third. I frowned at myself for mixing up percentages and vulgar fractions like that. I always did it, and I always frowned at myself for doing it, and then

I always worried about getting frown lines on my forehead if I kept on doing it, and then my life quickly spiraled away onto a whole other level of complication. I told myself I was only twenty-seven and that I didn't have any frown lines yet, and then I felt a little better. I half filled my glass. It was 50% full. Then I laughed at myself for being an idiot and taking everything way too seriously.

Even if we were perfect for each other, there was also a serious undercurrent of incompatibility at work. The affair was a major contributory factor, of course, but maybe it could be contextualised in terms of the ongoing stresses and strains caused by fluctuations in significant levels of underlying incompatibility. I wrote that down. Yes. That summed it up perfectly.

Maybe 'perfectly' was the wrong word.

I still had a third of a glass of wine left, so thought I might try filling in the Compatibility Index for a few of my other boyfriends. The ones that I didn't decide to marry. Not all of them asked, to be honest.

Callum Ellis didn't. He was only thirteen. He scored a lowly 24%, but there were a lot of questions about him that I couldn't really answer. Stuff about sex and career prospects mostly. We French kissed once. Sort of. He wanted to be an astronaut.

Ian Cruickshank scored 37%. I went out with him for a week because he had a leather jacket. No other reason.

Steve Hill scored 42%. I met Steve at university. He wrote poetry and wore eyeliner and thought it was cool to drink Pernod. He dropped out in the second year and wanted me to drop out with him and travel round the world in the back of a rusty camper van. I said no. He got as far as Devon before the camper van burst into flames on the hard shoulder of the A38 just outside Exeter. He works in software sales now.

I had a date with Bailey Southerton too. A long time ago. During a summer break. He lived in the village. He wasn't working for his father then. He scored 90%.

Dear Matilda

Just a quick note to say that washing machine No.76 is still with us – but only just. It was touch and go. Thankfully it has managed to pull through – so far. Bailey Southerton has already had to replace:

> *the water inlet valve*
> *the drive belt*
> *the heater element*
> *the heater element sensor*
> *bearings and seals*
> *2 drum paddles*
> *the door hinge*
> *the door release interlocker*
> *the drain pump*
> *and the control knob (twice)*

We have seen a great deal of him recently (!) He really is lovely. Always cheerful. Always polite. (Good-looking, too – don't tell your father I said that!) He says you were friends once. He sends his love. We all do. See you soon?

> *Love*
> *Mum x*

couch surfing

Jack was sleeping on Nadia's couch. He hadn't done anything wrong. He just couldn't sleep in the bed. Not yet. Jack wasn't ready. He wasn't used to it. He slept on couches. Any kind of couch really. Anywhere in the world. He could curl up on a small couch. Or put his feet over the edge. Or spread out on a big couch. Or make a nest of cushions on a couch that had extra cushions. Or make the most of a hard and uncomfortable couch. Yeah. Jack knew how to sleep on a couch. He needed time to acclimatise.

Nadia had a big bed. Huge. And circular. What was all that about? Who could sleep in a round bed? It was too much space for Jack to deal with. It had no edges. No orientation. He couldn't handle it. He'd get used to the idea, but for now he was still on the couch. He could sleep on a couch.

Jack wasn't asleep. Not anymore. He could hear slippers scuffing across the carpet towards him. He opened his eyes and smiled. Then he stopped smiling.

A man was standing over him. He was wearing a blue bathrobe tied at the waist and a pair of leather mules. He had a very hairy chest. He was carrying a small tray which he put down next to the couch. There were two mugs on the tray.

'I didn't know whether you liked tea or coffee, so I made both,' he said.

'Who are you?' Jack said.

'I'm Nadia's husband,' the man said, and flapped off across the floor.

5 things about Katherine

Katherine fell in love with a dentist. She didn't know that he was a dentist when she fell in love with him. There was no helping it. She always thought she would fall in love with a doctor. It was close enough.

Katherine bought handbags. It was okay for a while. Then it got out of hand. She promised not to buy any more handbags. She didn't. Then she bought handbags again. More promises. More handbags. One or the other.

Katherine bought handbags and stopped buying handbags and started buying them again long before she was told that she couldn't have children. It would be a mistake to think that the two things were linked in any way. They were not. Handbags were not a replacement or a substitute or an escape or a defense. They only became that afterwards.

Katherine knew that there was something beyond handbags and emptiness, but sometimes it was hard to see a way forward.

The Map of Us

Handbags had become a replacement and a substitute and an escape and a defense. The periods when she did not buy handbags became shorter. The number of handbags grew. The perfect handbag was her destination. Her husband did not understand. He did not believe that the perfect handbag was the answer. How could he? He was a dentist.

Katherine had a choice to make. Husband or handbags. It was not as simple as it sounded.

181

list

Katherine sat in her almost white living room at an imperceptibly white table and made a list. She didn't want to make a list, but she had to. She had all the information she required. It was all there. Nothing was missing.

It took her a day. There were columns to fill in. Positives and negatives. She tried to be as honest as she could. It would only work if she was honest.

She decided not to tell Clive about the list. Not until she was sure she could go through with it. What good would it do? When she was sure she would tell him. Only then.

Clive loved her. She had never doubted that for one minute. They had been married for ten years. He was constant and reliable and surprising and affectionate and not afraid to laugh at himself. He was a dentist and a contradiction and a rarity. He deserved better.

cluck

Katherine arranged to meet Barbara Maltravers in a small coffee shop that had a lunchtime tapas menu. They sat at a table near the back where they could not be seen from the street.

Barbara ordered a chamomile tea with a slice of fresh lemon. She ordered it in a cup, on a plain saucer, with a pot of extra hot water, and a warmed chocolate croissant with no icing sugar dusted on top, and two serviettes and a fork, and asked what the lunchtime specials were even though they were written on a chalkboard right in front of her and she clearly had no intention of staying for lunch.

Katherine ordered a flat white and left it at that. She took the list from a supermarket carrier bag and handed it across the table to Barbara. She didn't want to, but she knew that she had to. There was no alternative.

The completed list ran to 12 closely typed pages, stapled at the corner. It contained the details of 342 handbags in total. Average price: £372.50. Lowest price: £165. Most expensive single item: £2,380. She had two of them. With slightly different stitching. Tilly was the brains of the family, but Katherine was pretty good with numbers too.

Jules Preston

Barbara thumbed through the list making strange clucking sounds. Katherine knew that Barbara clucked. Every sales assistant in every handbag shop in London, New York, Paris and Milan knew that Barbara clucked too. She clucked when she was interested in buying something.

Barbara stopped clucking for a moment and carefully tore her croissant apart with a serviette in each hand, before swallowing a tiny morsel and washing it down with a sip of chamomile tea. Then she picked up the fork and used it to probe for non-existent crumbs trapped under her false fingernails.

'Who has seen this list?' Barbara asked, not looking up.

'Only you,' Katherine said.

'Only me?' Barbara said.

'I came to you first.'

Barbara clucked. She put the fork down.

'With original boxes?' she said.

'Yes.'

'All of them?'

'All of them.'

'Condition?'

'There's a column in the list. Mostly never used or mint,' Katherine said. 'I've tried to be as honest as I could.'

Barbara clucked. She picked the lemon out of her tea with the fork and started to chew the rind.

'Receipts?' Barbara said.

'Yes.'

'All of them?'

'All of them.'

184

Barbara finished the lemon and put the fork down again. She poured a little hot water into the saucer and dabbed her fingertips in it. She dried them on the serviettes using one for each hand.

'The price?' Barbara said.

'At the bottom of Page 12,' Katherine said.

Barbara flicked to the last page.

She clucked loudly.

'And that's for all of them?' Barbara said.

'Yes,' Katherine said. 'All of them.'

Barbara clucked. She didn't know that she clucked. It was a cluck that was about to save a marriage.

'Cash or cheque?' She said. Then she turned and reprimanded the waitress for misspelling 'chorizo' on the Specials Board.

olives

Matt and Grace were eating pizza. It was good pizza in a proper pizza restaurant. No side salads or pasta or garlic bread or chili oil. It wasn't a date. It was pizza. Grace was chasing olives around her plate, and Matt was trying to get cheese into his mouth without leaving strings of tomato sauce-covered mozzarella on his chin. It was hard to say who was having the most success.

Grace impatiently stabbed at a black olive with her fork only to watch it shoot off over the heads of the people on the next table. They were eating lasagna with a rocket and parmesan salad drizzled in a balsamic vinegar reduction. They were on a date. They didn't notice.

'She did what?' Grace said, trying to stifle a grin with about the same level skill as she had just employed to try and spear an olive.

'She wrote a report on our marriage,' Matt said, trying to twist cheese onto his fork like spaghetti. Round and round it went, making no discernible difference.

'That's outrageous,' Grace said, setting her sights on another unwary olive.

'She sent it to me. It has footnotes and a summary and a series of conclusions at the end,' Matt said as his continued cheese twisting threatened to lift all the topping off his pizza. Mushrooms, slices of pepperoni, extra onions – all caught up in the rubbery tangle.

'I can't believe it,' Grace said, pursuing an olive under the bits of crust she had piled up on the side of her plate for later.

'Our entire marriage is reduced to a series of numbers and diagrams,' Matt said, picking up his knife before the entire pizza ended up going down the front of his shirt.

'That's dreadful,' Grace said, sensing the time was right, aiming, stabbing, and watching another olive disappear across the restaurant. 'Can I read it?' she said.

3rd

Can't believe it.
Came third.
Disappointed.
Gutted.
Never come third.
Come second.
That's what I do.
Always.
Idiot.
Not for long though.
Half an hour.
Twenty minutes.
Maybe less.
Get called back.
Judges table packed away.
Chairs folded.
Tent taken down.
Important announcement.
Winner disqualified.

Donald Haddon.
Four times Regional Champion.
National finalist eight years in a row.
No wonder.
Secret pockets.
Sewn into his shorts.
Quick drying cement.
Same colour as the sand.
Can't believe it.
Donald Haddon disqualified.
I'm up to second.
Always come second.
Didn't feel like second.
Not proper second.
Didn't feel right.
Something in between.
Something less than second.
Second and a half.
Second and three quarters.
Tilly would know.
Draw a graph.
Upturned saucer.
Coloured pencils.
Tilly would know.
Donald Haddon disqualified.
Can't believe it.
Accountant.
Wife a social worker.

Jules Preston

Secret pockets sewn into his shorts.
Quick drying cement.
Same colour as the sand.
Why didn't I think of that?

layers

Daniel Bearing stood at the very doorstep of the vast Atlantic and knew without question that the Outer Hebrides was no place for a grey suit and matching socks. He got back in the car and drove a little east and then north until he was back at Stornoway. He parked the car outside an outdoor clothing shop in the town centre and hurried inside to get out of the rain.

He bought lightweight walking boots and a waterproof jacket and waterproof trousers and a waterproof coat with a hood. He bought two pairs of thick socks and a warm hat. He bought base layers and middle layers and outer layers, and changed in the shop. The sales assistant put his grey suit and white shirt and black tie and grey socks and handmade wingtip Oxfords in a large plastic bag and tried not to smirk at his misadventure until he had gone.

Daniel got back in the car and drove south and a little west for a second time. He was wearing so many layers he could barely move his arms.

silence

By the time Daniel got back to the house, it was dark. The door was not locked. He let himself in. He found a bedroom, and he went to sleep. There were nine bedrooms. It wasn't hard to find one. He had been traveling all day. It wasn't hard to sleep. He was bone-tired to start with.

It was the silence that eventually woke him. Not silence, but a lack of any noise that he understood. There was no traffic outside. The constant low-level hum of a restless city. All he could hear were waves.

S

Mrs Haddon was making phone calls. One after the other. Her phone had lots of buttons. Some of them lit up. Abby couldn't hear what Mrs Haddon was saying. She was talking quietly. It was 7.26pm. It was dark outside. Abby wanted to go home.

Mrs Haddon was interested in Abby's book. She opened it at the start. She held it open while she wrote something down on a pad with a pen that didn't work. She chose another pen. That didn't work either. She found a pencil. It was broken. She dialed a number. Abby didn't hear what she said.

Mrs Haddon put the phone down and drew a ring around something on the pad with a pen that barely left a mark. She picked up the phone again and dialed a new number. Nothing happened for a while. Then someone answered.

'Yes. Hello?' She said. 'I'm sorry to bother you. My name is Mrs Haddon. I'm a social worker. I was hoping that you might be able to help me. This is going to sound like an odd question. Are you related to a David North? He had a sister called Violet. Yes. You are? I'm sorry. There's been an accident.'

Abby knew then that she wasn't going home. She was never going home. She was going somewhere else. She did not know where. It was easier for her mum that way.

walls

Violet had encountered a new problem. One that she had not foreseen. How could she? She was dealing with a landscape entirely of her own imagination. It had no centre. No true north. No direction for the sun to rise and set. It had no city to the west or rugged coastline to the south. It was set adrift in a somewhere that was still not fully resolved.

She had been lucky so far. At no point did 'Walks from Shiny Brook to Burton Hole' cross the path of 'Walks from Black Lake to Tin Gate Mire.' They were many miles apart. Or were they? Violet did not know. She had not thought of it until now.

How would Arthur Galbraith get from the end of one walk to the start of another? How could the two be joined? It was a puzzle of small pieces in a picture that was still in the process of growing. Not unsolvable as yet, but as the number of volumes grew it would soon become impossible for one piece not to fall awkwardly upon another.

The Great Moor could not stretch away forever. That would not do. Never returning to a familiar place by a different route. Never seeing a known landmark from a different angle or as a dark shape looming on a distant horizon. It must stop somewhere. It required a chart. A map. Something that would bring it together. Make it real. It was clear that it could not go on without one.

Violet sat back in her chair. The study was not a large room. There was a window that looked out onto the garden. There was desk and a typewriter and a bookshelf. There was a fireplace. The walls were bare. Her family had taken the picture frames when they left. And the curtains and the lamp-shades and the door handles.

The walls were bare. Yes. She would paint a map of the Great Moor on the walls. She would add the details as she went. Then she would never be lost again.

map

Violet started the map at Tin Gate Mire. It was a place that she had made a sketch of. It was in the second book. It was a flat piece of waterlogged land in the trough of a shallow valley. There was only one safe path through the mire. Few went by that way. There were tall reeds and biting flies and stagnant pools of peat-brown water that were deeper than they seemed. It was easier to make the journey around than through. It took twice as long. That was the price that most agreed to pay.

The mire was 12 miles from Black Lake. Black Lake was to the west. Violet put the mire directly above the fireplace. It was as good a place to start as any. She kept it small and marked in the direction followed by the valley in thin lines of paint. The paint was dark brown. Owen had found it for her. He found brushes too that he had extended so that she did not have to reach up too far.

Violet was wearing her least favourite dress. It was hard to choose. She had no dress she truly liked. They were all old and chosen for her by her mother. She did not care if any of them became covered in paint.

Jules Preston

Violet decided that the size of her hand would account for a mile. There was no point finding a more accurate ruler. She would always have her hands with her. They would suffice. She measured twelve hands to her left and marked a place for Black Lake. She remembered the shape of the water from her description in the first chapter of the book. She painted it in with deft strokes. The long-handled paintbrushes were lighter and easier to use than they appeared.

The woodland and fields that surrounded the lake she knew well. Arthur Galbraith had sat and admired the view for some time before setting off towards Tin Gate Head and the valley beyond.

The dog watched Violet from the doorway. It was raining outside.

home

The dog was investigating his new home. He climbed the stairs. Slowly at first. Then at a steady gallop. He stopped at the first-floor landing where the carpet ended. He did not know what to make of it.

There was a bathroom ahead of him. He ignored it. He looked up through the stairwell to where the spindles were broken and missing. He bared his teeth. No one saw him do it. There was something up there that he did not like. He decided to go no further. He went back downstairs.

There was a front parlour and a wide hallway and a study and a kitchen, and he examined them all. The tiles in the hallway were slick and cold. The kitchen floor was no better. The front parlour was seldom in use. He would be left in peace there. He was not a dog who found the idea of tranquility appealing.

There was nothing for him upstairs. He would not go there again. There was no one there. He could tell. He could smell it. They could not fool him. It was something else. Something left behind.

He found a place for himself under her desk in the study.

She was still painting the walls. He would not be in the way.
He could be close to her there. He wanted that more than
anything.

petunias

I have never used a typewriter. My grandmother did. My mother did, too. They used the same typewriter. A turquoise blue Royal Quiet Deluxe that was originally borrowed from a neighbour.

It was borrowed from Mrs Gladys Everson. She lived in a house across the road that was much the same as Violet's except it had a small garden that was paved and had flowers in pots and hanging baskets. Many years later her husband would back his caravan over my tortoise and solve my disagreement with '3' and '5.' Maybe the timing was just a coincidence.

He said it was an accident. The tortoise used to get into their garden and eat the French lavender. And the geraniums. And the potted hostas. And the forget-me-nots. And especially the petunias. He had been returned to us several times. Mr Everson used to scoop him up with a brass coal shovel and deposit him on our front step.

He used the same brass shovel to scrape the flattened tortoise from his driveway.

Violet eventually bought the typewriter from Mrs Everson. We did not live there then. We lived there later.

When Violet bought the typewriter, Mr Everson did not have a caravan – though he was already considering buying one. There were no tortoises in his garden. He was proud of his French lavender. And the geraniums. And the potted hostas. And the forget-me-nots. And especially the petunias.

He already had the brass coal shovel though. He used it to flick slugs and snails into Violet's garden.

lucky

When my grandmother's health began to fail, she did not move in with us. We moved in with her. I was two. I do not remember her well. My sister and brother knew her better. They were older. Katherine can remember my grandfather. She says she can.

When I was four or five I was allowed into my grandmother's study for the first time. I saw the painted walls. The map of the Great Moor. From floor to ceiling. Around the window. Over the fireplace. The land of Arthur Galbraith. I would often stand in the doorway and stare. Sometimes I still do.

We all chose to have rooms on the second floor. The third floor was not a place that felt welcoming. My mother said that it was where Violet's brother had once lived.

I go home when I can. Not as often as I would like. I have my own flat. Matt and I bought it together. I bought most of it. Matt said he would help with the mortgage. He was a lot less help than anticipated.

I decided it was time that I saw my father. If I was lucky, maybe I would run into Bailey Southerton too.

snoring

The house was cool and empty. My father was not at home. The back door was open. I went out into the garden. It was not how it was when my grandfather was alive. The man with one name. The man who turned up sometime in June with a spade and a dog and decided by December that he could not leave again. Love would not let him go.

The paths were overgrown. The borders were neglected. I wish I had met him. He died before I was born.

I could hear snoring. I walked towards the sound. It was familiar and strangely comforting. Sidney was sitting in the shade of the large apple tree. If you asked him he would say that he was not asleep. No. Not at all. He was a retired solicitor, so it was best not to argue.

That makes him sound severe and unapproachable. Nothing could be further from the truth. He was a short, stout man with a moustache that had been his constant companion since he was a teenager. He came from hirsute stock. His own father had a single bushy eyebrow that grew uninterrupted from one temple to the other and was clearly the source of his cascading side whiskers. I never got to meet it in person, but I have seen photographs. His eyebrow was a triumph.

Sidney was a very dear friend. A kind and generous and secretive man. We all regard him as a member of the family – and we always will.

company

I went back into the house and made a pot of tea. Sidney knew the whistle of the kettle well. It would give him the opportunity to open his eyes in peace.

I put the pot and cups and two saucers on a tray, poured milk into a small jug and returned to the garden.

'Matilda,' he said when he saw me coming. He was fully awake now.

Yes. I was wrong. It was not just my mother who called me that. It was Sidney, too.

He smiled, happy of the company.

We sat in the shade of the apple tree and drank tea and watched the bees go about their business and did not talk much. Sidney is ninety-two. He has lost the sense of words now. At first it frustrated him. Then he was frightened. Now he could no longer describe how he felt. He had not fallen silent though. He hummed and sang and clicked as if his tongue was not yet ready to rest. His eyes had lost none of their mischief.

Sidney sipped his tea. His leather gloves creaked. The grey

tips of his moustache were wet. He was still there. Only his words had gone missing.

I heard an old car pull up. It was French and full of sand. I did not need to see it to know.

wonderful

I left Sidney in the shade of the apple tree and went back inside.

My father's sand sculpting tools were already piled in the kitchen sink. The cold tap was running. There was a 2nd Place trophy on the table. It was about four inches tall and the shape of a sandcastle with the word 'Winner!' written emphatically on the side. My father was standing up eating vanilla ice cream direct form the tub with a large serving spoon. There was a trail of sand on the floor. He was wearing a white T-shirt and knee-length khaki shorts and open toed sandals. His feet were brown, but only where his toes poked through. He had tan lines where the straps of his sandals crossed over. He had thin, muscular arms, and he wore his wedding ring on a piece of blue baler twine tied around his neck. Always. My father has looked much the same for almost every moment that I can remember.

'Who came first?' I asked.

'Bloody dolphins,' he said through a mouthful of ice cream.

I got another spoon from the drawer and joined him. I had to scrape a fine dusting of sand off the top of the ice cream first.

'Sidney is here,' I said.

'Sidney? How wonderful.'

My father thought that everything was wonderful. The difference was in the pronunciation. The cadence of his voice. He had a special 'wonderful' that was reserved for Sidney alone. It was subtle and hard to explain. It had a great deal of joy in it.

'I saw Jack,' I said.

'I know. He called. He's coming down to see me in a few days. Maybe you could come as well.'

A 'maybe' from my father meant that I was coming whatever. But in a nice way.

'He was with someone,' I said, trying not to overemphasize the 'someone' too much.

'I know.' He glanced sideways at me and smiled. 'How wonderful,' he said.

5 things about my father

There was a sandpit in a playground in a park in the broken heart of the city. There were swings and a tall slide and a not-so-tall slide and a cafe that was always closed. It was a wooden hut with a window where you could buy ice lollies and cans of drink and crisps. But you couldn't because it was always closed. It had a big sign outside telling you all the prices of the things it sold, but it didn't. There were always half a dozen pigeons sunning themselves on the roof. Or sometimes a seagull. But the seagulls never stuck around long because the cafe was always closed and there wasn't anything to eat. The seagulls would fly off, and within minutes half a dozen pigeons would return as if they had never been away. None of that mattered to my father. He was in the sandpit.

There was a blue spade at first. It was plastic. It was left in the sandpit by someone else. There were probably tears when it was lost. Or maybe it was forgotten. Or maybe they took another spade home that they thought was a better spade and left the blue spade in its place. There were probably tears

210

for the better spade. Whatever that spade was. Or maybe the spade was a gift. Maybe it was a parting gift that said:

'I have played in this sandpit, but now it is time for me to grow up and stop playing with sand and sandpits and spades and get a proper job – like going to school and learning things that might be useful at some as yet undetermined time in the future of my life. Have this spade and remember me, for I was here and built sandcastles and waited for the cafe to open but it never did. Goodbye.' It did not matter how the blue plastic spade first appeared there. My father made good use of it.

There was a day that it rained. There was a thin layer of wet sand on top of the dry sand beneath. My father built tunnels with paper thin ceilings.

There was a day when all the sand was wet. As far down as you could dig. It was winter. The park was empty. The playground was locked and chained. My father climbed the fence and built a sandcastle that was as tall as he could reach.

Then there was a day when my father was told to leave the sandpit and let the children play in it. He had been there long enough. He had learned everything he needed to know.

old flame

A van pulled up outside the house just as I was leaving. It had 'Southerton Electrical Appliances' written on the side. It was another new washing machine being delivered. A man climbed out of the cab. He was tall with broad shoulders and an easy smile and a familiar mop of dark curly hair. I stopped in my tracks.

'Bailey,' I said.

'Tilly,' he said.

He walked towards me and took my hand. It was warm and strong. He laughed. It was a sound that instantly reignited something deep inside me that I thought had gone out long ago.

Then he told me about his beautiful wife and two young children, and it fizzled out again for good.

art school

Jack didn't wait for Nadia to explain. He just left. He threw on his clothes, tied his shoelaces and was out of the door in minutes.

The street was familiar. It was a part of the city that he knew.

Jack called Moss. She was an old friend from Art School. Her flat was nearby. She wouldn't ask too many questions. She was a chef now. She used onion skins and celery leaves in stock. She could crack eggs just by looking at them. She had a kitchen the size of a cupboard that was crammed with tins and dried herbs and jars of spices that looked like soil samples from alien planets. Her favourite colour was green. She was safe. She had a couch that could be trusted.

She didn't answer. She was out. It wasn't a problem. Jack knew where she hid the key.

bijou

Jack let himself in. Moss's kitchen was the size of a cupboard. The rest of her flat was no bigger. It had two small rooms. One had a bed. The other had a couch. The room with the couch was called the living room. It was deeply ironic. There was a large mirror that was supposed to make everything look bigger and more spacious. It didn't. There was a note stuck to the frame. It had Jack's name on it.

'Jack. In case you should drop by. No hot water. Have to turn the immersion heater on. Switch by the cooker. Clean towels under the sink. Beer in the fridge. If not, go and buy some. Slacker. Back at 8. x'

Jack sat on the couch and thought about Nadia. Then he got up and looked in the fridge. It was a little early to look in the fridge. There were no beers. He sat back down on the couch. Then he got up went out to buy beers. Five seconds later he let himself back in and turned the immersion heater on and found a clean towel under the sink. The he went out for a second time to buy beers.

In all the time he was in the flat he had probably walked six feet.

view

Moss got back to her flat at 8pm. She found Jack asleep on the couch. He had a towel wrapped around his waist. She admired the view for a moment. Then she looked in the fridge. There were beers. Two different kinds. Italian and Spanish. Bottles, not cans. There was barely room for anything else. It was a small fridge.

She took out a beer. It was ice cold. It was a small fridge, but it knew its stuff. She opened the bottle and admired the view a bit more. Jack really didn't look like a world authority on the colour blue. He looked like he owned a skateboard. She knew that he got that a lot. It was true though.

Moss thought about cooking something. She had been cooking all day. She was tired of cooking. Jack could cook. She could wake him up and make him do it.

Waking him up would mean that she wouldn't be able to admire the view anymore. Maybe she'd wake him up when she finished the beer. Yeah. It was a big bottle. It was ice cold. She could make it last.

colour

The door to Katherine's handbag room had been left open. It seemed strange. It was a door that was always locked. Clive was curious. He had never been inside before. He knew that the room was a variant of white and that there were glass shelves and adjustable lights and row upon row of expensive handbags. He didn't know how many. He didn't want to know. He didn't want to look. Then he looked.

The glass shelves were empty. The handbags were gone. He didn't know where. He didn't smile. It wasn't any kind of victory. He simply nodded.

Katherine had done her part. Now it was his turn.

Clive went into the approximately white kitchen and found the drawer where he had hidden them - all the colour charts that his wife had given him over the years. Dozens of them. Full of zesty greens and rich caramels. Cool neutrals and warm reds. It was going to be hard. White was his favourite colour. But he had to try.

He picked up the first chart. 'Burnt Orange and Soft Russet.' Then the next.

Anything but blue, he thought. *Anything but blue.*

overlap

When I got home, I drew a diagram. It was more of a scribble, really. I entitled it 'Why I Didn't Notice That Bailey Southerton Was 90% Compatible Until It Was Already Seven and a Half Years Too Late.'

Yes. I know. I have a problem with overly long titles for things. I should have called it something concise and pithy, but I really don't think that way. I think overly long and a little bit boring. I always have. I did try to abbreviate the title, but that just made it long and completely meaningless.

WIDNTBSW90%CUIWASAAHYTL

See what I mean? I rubbed it out. It was harder than I thought. I was using a purple pencil.

It turned into a sort of Venn diagram with two circles that barely met in the middle. They only overlapped for a few days one summer almost eight years ago. It was my opportunity to be with Bailey Southerton and be happy forever, and I missed it. I wrote that down with an arrow pointing at the intersection. Then I abbreviated it.

MOTBWBSABHFAIMI

I left it on the page. I didn't try and rub it out this time.

Then I drew a large broken heart in pen with lots of little arrows sticking out of it from different angles. Then I drew some more cracks in the heart. Then even more arrows. Then I stopped before I messed it up.

The diagram wasn't strictly part of my report, but I put it in the lever arch folder anyway. I hadn't put anything new in the folder for weeks. Diagrams are great.

pie

I like pie charts. A pie chart can reveal a great deal about a relationship. Seriously. A pie chart is simple to draw and easy to understand, and you can colour them in. I like that part best.

Pie charts are good for proportions. Things that are clearly unequal, like who uses the three-seater sofa most or does the least amount of housework or pays less than their fair share of the bills. A pie chart will show you that. There is no argument with a pie chart.

I draw pie charts by drawing around an upturned saucer. I divide the circle into four and then eight using faint pencil lines. I mark out the proportions as accurately as I can, and then I colour them in. I only need two colours. I am always red. Matt is always yellow.

The red pencil is soft and easy to colour with. The yellow pencil is hard and gritty and breaks a lot and needs sharpening and sometimes leaves a much harder line than it should. I have tried holding the pencil close to the tip and using small, equal strokes. It makes no difference. The pie chart for 'Three-

Seater Sofa Usage' took me an hour. There was a lot of yellow to get through.

I did the red first. It was a very small slice of pie.

blip

For things that happen over a period of time, you really need a line graph. They're good for identifying trends. Line graphs are okay, but they don't have the same capacity for colouring-in as pie charts. You can use lots of different coloured lines if you want to, but it's not the same. Line graphs can be highly informative as long as you get the timescale right. For 'Sexual Activity' I chose to use *per month*. *Per week* was a little too ambitious, and I didn't have reliable figures. Maybe I should have kept a diary?

There was meteoric rise at the start, as was to be expected, then a small plateau appeared between three and six months before reportable sexual activity plummeted to a fortnightly blip, every other Friday night after the pub quiz. There was a significant revival of activity before and after the wedding, but within two months it had returned to the blip again. Then the blip changed to every other Wednesday when they changed the night of the quiz.

I tried to be consistent with what qualified as sexual activity, too. Even when an hour or so of fumbling with bra straps and shoelaces and a back massage and some holding hands afterwards was replaced by a quickie on the sofa and an apologetic kiss on the neck.

perspective

'I think the line graph for "Sexual Activity" is misleading and grossly inaccurate,' Matt said.

'I think it's the "Three-Seater Sofa Usage" where you really let yourself down,' Grace said.

'You think so?' Matt said.

'I wouldn't put up with it,' Grace said.

'Wouldn't you?'

'Not for a moment. You didn't even pay for your half.'

'How do you know that?' Matt said.

'I read the footnotes.' Grace said, sarcastically.

'What page is that?'

Grace kicked the wire sprung mattress above her head.

'How did someone so utterly dim get the top bunk?' she said.

'I gave you my duvet, didn't I?' Matt said.

The duvet had steam trains on it. Streetlight was shining through the football curtains. Grace was counting the green florescent stars stuck to the ceiling and wondering why there were little holes in the plaster and the spaceship wallpaper was torn.

'Who is that singing?' she asked.

'That's mum.' Matt said.

'Does she always sing like that?' Grace said.

'Only when she's in love,' Matt said, putting the report down and making hand shadow shapes on the door with his torch. They were all variations on a barking dog, but some of them had antlers.

'What do you do when you're in love?' Grace said.

Matt peered over the edge of the bed.

'Do you want me to come down there and show you?' he said.

Grace smiled.

'Forget that. I'm coming up,' she said.

And she did.

transformation

Daniel found his father on the beach. He did not recognise him. His father was wearing a T-shirt and rolled up jeans. He had bare feet. He was leaning on the hull of an upturned boat reading a newspaper. There were two mugs of coffee perched on the keel.

'I heard you arrive,' his father said. 'Wondered when you were going to wake up. You've been asleep for two days.'

Daniel was shocked. He didn't know what to say. He was thirty years old, and he had never seen his father wearing anything but a grey suit. Something had changed.

twit

Daniel stood on the beach in his waterproof coat and his waterproof trousers and his thick socks and his warm hat and looked at his father wearing rolled up jeans and a T-shirt and felt like a right twit.

'Why are you here?' his father asked.

'I wanted to see you,' Daniel said.

His father put his newspaper down.

'Why are you really here?' he said.

'I needed a break,' Daniel said.

His father handed him a mug of coffee.

'Try again,' his father said.

'I'm tired,' Daniel said.

'Now we're getting somewhere,' his father said, picking seaweed from between his toes.

'I met someone, and I watched her leave, and I did nothing about it,' Daniel said. 'I should have called her, but I didn't know what to say.'

His father thought for a moment.

'I'd better find you some jeans and a T-shirt then,' he said. 'You look like a right twit.'

SW

Abby was sitting in the back of Mrs Haddon's car. She had her seatbelt on. Her school bag was on the seat beside her. They had been driving for hours. They had stopped on the way. Mrs Haddon just had coffee. Abby had chips and ketchup. The chips were thin chips. Then they got back in the car.

Mrs Haddon was like a teacher. She didn't say much. When she did speak she was telling things. Abby just nodded or shook her head. It didn't matter which.

Mrs Haddon had short hair. Not as short as Abby's. Mrs Haddon's hair was grey and straight and pushed behind her ears. Mrs Haddon's hair needed washing. Abby had short hair, so it didn't need washing. It was easier for her mum. Abby wanted a fringe. She couldn't have one.

They were going slower now. They were almost there. Abby didn't go in cars often, but she knew what going slower meant. Abby had never been in a car for so long. Johnnie Gilbert was always sick in a car if he went in it for so long. He told her. He told everyone how sick he got on the way to France. He was so sick they had to change his clothes and give him a bucket to hold under his chin and let him ride in the front with the window open. Johnnie Gilbert was always telling stories about sick.

Mrs Haddon stopped the car outside a house. There were lights on inside. The house was white.

extortion

It is by no means clear how the North family became aware of Violet's change in fortune. But they did. It took them eight years. They had lost hope of her falling and dying in any way that was convenient to them. They had lost hope and forgotten her almost completely. And then they chose to forget no longer. They were drawn back. It was not compassion or regret or forgiveness or reconciliation that drew them. No. They took a much straighter path. Greed.

Her brother, David North, a cruel young man grown from a cruel young boy, drove slowly past on some pretext. Then he stopped. Not directly outside, but further down the road where he could not be seen.

He found the house to be in good repair and the large garden immaculately kept. He left his car and made enquiries in the village where he was not remembered. Violet was to be married and had six published volumes to her name. Her husband-to-be was kind and devoted. They had a dog.

It was true then. David felt sick to his dark soul. The family had been tricked.

He drove home. He did not interrupt his mother with the

news, for she was not currently accepting visitors. He helped his father write a letter that they sent the same day. They demanded £20,000 for the house with the large garden and expected immediate payment in due course.

To oversee the legalities of the extortion they chose to retain the services of a solicitor.

In that regard, they chose most unwisely.

4lb 11oz

David North had always been frightened of his sister. Her frail legs bothered him. He especially disliked the thick leather straps and tight buckles of her leg braces. The metal support rods, hinged at the knee, attached to a plain shoe with rivets. The strange, lopsided laces offset at an angle. He would not go near them. He thought they looked like scissors.

He had his bedroom on the third floor of the house. He was beyond and above the limit of her adventure. He could hide from her if he wanted. But hiding and worrying did not suit his disposition. He would watch her through the fluted spindles of the staircase. Disgusted, fearful and fascinated. He took to breaking the spindles out and dropping them on her down the stairwell. He soon realised that sawing the spindles nearly in half first and then breaking them against the skirting board made long, sharp splinters. He took to dropping those instead until his father discovered him and he was punished for using the saw without permission.

David thought the punishment was unjust. He found other things to drop instead. Heavy things. Books. He had a favourite. A dictionary. Bound in red leather with gold embossed lettering. Volume VI: 'L to N.' It weighed 4lb 11oz. If he missed, he would run down the stairs and retrieve it.

There were three flights and a small landing. He would be silent. He would wait for Violet to pass beneath him again. He was patient and determined. He hit her with the book many times. She fell and got up again.

David's father was displeased. He encouraged him to use Volume VII: 'O and P' instead. It weighed more.

Juniper

Violet opened the door to a short, stout man wearing a herringbone suit and a jaunty hat. He had a moustache and mischievous eyes and a handkerchief stuffed in his jacket pocket that was not entirely virgin cloth. Violet noticed these things. He carried an alligator skin Gladstone bag that had not been worn by an alligator in some time.

The short, stout, mischievous-eyed man smiled and held out a gloved hand.

'It is a great pleasure to meet you,' he said and stepped inside without invitation.

Violet entertained the unexpected visitor in the front parlour. Owen was aware of his presence but remained in the garden.

'My name is Mr Charles S. Juniper,' the man said, sipping tea from a delicate porcelain cup with his gloves on. 'I apologise for the intrusion, but I wanted to see things for myself before proceeding any further.'

He took another sip of tea. His leather gloves creaked. The tips of his moustache were wet. For the briefest of moments his eyes skipped across Violet's legs and took in the well-worn

233

buckles and metal rods of her leg braces. He looked up. 'Forgive me,' he said. 'I see now that everything your family have told me about you is of course entirely untrue. As I suspected.'

'Thank you,' said Violet, without any idea what she was actually thanking him for.

He put his cup down but made no effort to remove his gloves.

'Let us start again,' he said. 'My name is Mr Charles S. Juniper, as I have mentioned already. Now that we are friends I can tell you that the "S" stands for Sidney. You may call me Charles or Sidney, but please not Charlie.'

Violet nodded.

'Do not be alarmed, but I am a solicitor. I am a junior partner in the firm of Twelvetrees, Juniper and Brompton of 14a Sneed Street, London. The "Juniper" in the title belongs to my father, not me. I hope one day to make him proud. I have done little so far to believe that my hopes will be rewarded.'

Violet stirred her tea. She had no need to. It was already well stirred and contained no sugar. It was merely an occupation for her hands.

'I must inform you that I have recently been retained by members of your estranged family to deal with your purchase of this house.'

Violet sat forward.

Mr Juniper sat forward too and lifted a solitary gloved finger.

'But,' he said. 'I have just decided to return their deposit. I will not be taking the case after all.'

Violet was confused.

Then Mr Juniper opened his ancient alligator bag and produced three worn volumes of *Galbraith's Boot*, including a copy of the first edition. He smiled warmly.

'I am a very great fan, and I am your humble servant,' he said. He took a gold fountain pen from his pocket and held out the books towards her.

'As I may have mentioned. To Charles or Sidney, but please not Charlie.'

5 things about the Norths

It did not take Mr Juniper long to discover that Violet's house did not belong to the North family at all. It was not theirs to sell. It had never been theirs. It was rented. They had not paid the rent. Not in all the time they had lived there. The true owner was in no position to protest. His name was Mr Lawrence Cradlethorpe. He had suffered a long and debilitating illness brought on by a prodigious capacity for tawny port. When his liver finally packed its bags, he promptly expired without leaving a coherent will. All that remained was a thin document fraught with inconsistencies that became the subject of endless legal wrangling between distant relatives scattered randomly throughout the furthest corners of the world. The house and its defaulting tenants were quickly and utterly forgotten.

Violet's father was a man called Michael North. He had convictions for theft, fraud and embezzlement. He had other names too. He had no genuine profession. He was at some point a doctor and an industrialist and an inventor and a philanthropist and a famous sportsman and an exiled heir to a foreign throne. In all things he was a practiced and eloquent liar. He had debts and made enemies. Michael North had a bony face and blunt hands and knew how to put both to good use if he had to.

Violet had a younger brother called David. He was a weasel. Thin as a paperclip. He had little in the way of formal education. No school could hold him for long. He took after his father's ways. He lived beyond his means and stayed in hotel rooms that he had no intention of paying for. David North was a young man with no prospects and little future. If he had a coin in his pocket, it was someone else's.

Violet's mother was a mystery. She seemed barely to exist. Mr Juniper was led to believe that she was still alive, but he could find no description of her. There was no certificate of her birth or record of her marriage to Michael North. He did not know what part she played in all of this. If any. Her name was Pearl or Mary. No one seemed certain which.

The whereabouts of the North family was equally tantalising. David was in London. Somewhere. Staying in a hotel that would find his bed unmade and the towels all missing in the morning. Michael had an address in Birmingham. It was a boarded-up warehouse next to a cemetery. Pearl or Mary could be anywhere. Who would know it was her?

£1,000

Mr Charles S. Juniper arrived at the offices of solicitors Truelove & Pynche shortly before noon. He did not have an appointment. He gave the secretary his card and was asked to wait. He found a chair that was comfortable enough and sat upon it for no more than five minutes with his Gladstone bag held securely on his lap. Then he was ushered into the private office of Mr Benjamin Pynche, a tall man with a pronounced stoop and a poorly maintained goatee. It was sparse and grey and nothing like Mr Juniper's impeccable moustache.

'How may I be of service?' Mr Pynche asked, turning Mr Juniper's card over in his hand.

'On the contrary. I was hoping that I could be of some service to you,' Mr Juniper said, sitting in the chair that was offered to him and placing his Gladstone bag carefully on the floor at his feet. Mr Pynche made note of the care with which it was put down – just as Mr Juniper knew he would.

'How so?' Mr Pynche said flatly. He was a solicitor being offered an accommodation by another solicitor. A solicitor who wore leather gloves indoors. He had every right to be suspicious.

'I believe your firm are the principal executors for the estate of the late Mr Lawrence Cradlethorpe,' Mr Juniper said. Mr Pynche stroked his ramshackle goatee nervously – just as Mr Juniper knew he would.

'Yes,' Mr Pynch said, not wanting to say any more until he knew what this was all about.

'For the last twenty-three years in fact?' Mr Juniper said.

'Yes,' Mr Pynche said.

'And how is the matter progressing?'

'Slowly,' Mr Pynche said wearily. 'There are several claims and counterclaims and few serviceable assets to go around.'

'Indeed,' Mr Juniper said soothingly.

'And what is your involvement in this?' Mr Pynche asked – just as Mr Juniper knew he would.

'I represent a client that is interested in purchasing an asset belonging to the estate. A property that I believe has been overlooked and is of little consequence,' Mr Juniper said. He reached down into his Gladstone bag and pulled out a stack of bright pink ten pound notes held together with a large elastic band. He placed the money on Mr Pynche's desk.

'One thousand pounds,' Mr Juniper said. 'You may count it if you wish, but I can assure you there is no need. I would like to conclude the purchase as a matter of urgency.'

Mr Juniper could hear Mr Pynche's stomach rumbling – just as he knew it would. It was why he had attended the offices of Truelove & Pynche at noon. It was lunchtime. Mr Pynch was being offered a great deal of money. Of course his stomach would rumble at the thought. Lunchtime was always a good time to tempt the hungry.

'It may take some time to draw up the necessary papers,' Mr Pynche said.

Mr Juniper reached down into his Gladstone bag again and pulled out a series of legal documents.

'I have saved you the trouble,' Mr Juniper said. 'I also have a copy of the freehold title deeds in case you were unable to find them. Please take a few moments to review the agreement and then sign where I have marked with a cross.'

Mr Pynche glanced from Mr Juniper to the pile of used banknotes on his desk. Perhaps he could distribute a small amount to each claimant and set aside the remainder to cover his own costs.

Mr Pynche's stomach rumbled.

The house belonged to Violet – just as Mr Juniper knew it would.

important

It was Wednesday night. I was sitting on the floor in the living room. I was leaning against the wall because the sofa had finally gone. I was surrounded by a rectangle of inch-thick dusty pink fluff, dotted with pen tops and torn edges of sweet wrappers and a receipt for a pint of milk and a lump of congealed brown rice and a scrap of paper with 'Your Mum Called. Can You Ring Her Back? It's Important' written on it, which I had never seen before. It was definitely time for some therapeutic chocolate.

Matt didn't believe in the medicinal powers of chocolate. I did. I guess that was part of our problem right there. Chocolate had all sorts of curative qualities that were not easy to substantiate. When Matt was around I used to have to justify my chocolate intake on a daily basis. Not that I actually ate chocolate on a daily basis. Not all the time, anyway.

I used to have to say things like:

'It's not what it looks like.'

Which was classic denial, or:

'I'm not eating it all.'

Which would probably turn out to be a lie, or:

'Leave me alone.'

Which was just infantile and annoying. Or, my own personal favourite:

'I didn't expect you back so soon.'

Which usually meant that I hadn't managed to finish the entire bar before he barged in and caught me.

Now that Matt had gone, I didn't have to justify eating chocolate anymore, so I've been eating a lot of bananas. It's probably better for me.

Matt liked to think that he had the moral high ground. He thought that he was health-conscious because he walked to the corner shop and didn't take the car. The fact that he couldn't drive the car didn't seem to enter into his thinking.

I sat on the floor in a rectangle of dusty pink fluff. It was like the ghost of the sofa was still there. I hadn't vacuumed under it since we moved into the flat. I leant against the wall and looked at the note again. 'Your Mum Called. Can You Ring Her Back? It's Important.'

I cried and ate chocolate too. Chocolate is good, but it doesn't work all the time.

Dear Matilda

Just a quick note to say that washing machine No.76 is sadly no longer with us. Bailey Southerton said he had replaced nearly every part that he could. He said that it held on valiantly to the very end. Using the half load function may have extended its life for a little longer, but only for a matter of days. When the time came there was really nothing more that he could do. He took it away in his van and hopes to have a replacement here by the end of the week. No doubt there are new washing machines in a warehouse somewhere trembling in their boxes at the very thought.

Your father has decided he is going to build a sandpit in the garden. Apparently he needs more practice. As if he doesn't spend enough time covered in sand already. And dragging it into the house and killing off defenseless washing machines. He just has to decide where to put it. Sidney said he didn't mind where it went as long as it wasn't anywhere near the apple tree. He didn't actually say that, but you could tell that he wanted to. Sidney has been humming a lot recently.

Katherine is acting strangely again. I don't know how Clive puts up with her. I suppose she does let him paint everything white.

Your brother has disappeared. Not uncommon for Jack. No doubt he is doing something deeply blue.

I have been feeling a little odd recently. I haven't

mentioned it to anyone. It will probably go away on its own. Just getting old I suppose. It would be wonderful to see you. Wonderful? I sound like your father.

Love you
Mum x

rivers

I re-read mum's letters often. They are full of sand and broken washing machines and handbags and things that are blue.

She always wrote letters. She wrote them in Violet's study. She would move the turquoise blue Royal Quiet Deluxe typewriter aside and write with the dip pen and ink that her mother once used to draw sketches of the Great Moor.

Mum's handwriting had been shaped by the nib of the dip pen since she was child. There were no hard edges or sudden changes of direction. It was joined up and flowing with a distinct forward lean.

You could tell where on the study walls she had taken over the painting of the Moor from her mother. The names had a flourish. The letters were more playful and precise. Mum excelled at painting rivers. The river Haresfoot that flows underneath the window and around the bookshelf is my favourite. There are rapids and a waterfall. There is a trout jumping, and an otter. Violet had the edge when it came to mountains and valleys. They were both expert at bridges and stone circles.

Jules Preston

Mum rarely said anything about feeling ill. Then she stopped writing.

unexpected

Good sand.
Quality sand.
Sand I've never seen before.
Wasn't-here-last-week sand.
Who would have thought it possible sand.
Sand where sand doesn't belong.
Sand where shingle was only yesterday.
Sand where shingle has always been.
Unexpected sand.
Storm sand.
Rough weather sand.
Sand brought here.
Sand that is on its way to somewhere else.
Doesn't-know-where sand.
Temporary sand.
Stopping-off sand.
Have-to-be-quick sand.
May-not-be-here-tomorrow sand.
Catch-me-now sand.
One-day-only sand.

Jules Preston

Pale yellow sand.
Roll-it-in-your-hand sand.
Better than your average sand.
Sand with character.
Sand with ambition.
Sand with purpose.
Sand that has something to say for itself.
Sand that means something.
Good sand.
Not trying-to-trick-you sand.
Not full-of-shells sand.
Good sand.
Goodbye sand.
I can't.
Not now.
There is no time.
She needs me.

matches

Matt had a warm coat and a starlit night and a large box of matches and the keys to a scaffolding yard that belonged to a friend who didn't mind him burning stuff as long as he locked up afterwards.

Grace was there, too. She helped him unload the sofa from the back of the hire van. It was heavier than it looked. Matt removed the copy of 'Elementary Statistics and the Role of Randomness' that stopped the sofa from rocking backwards. It was time. The sofa was toast.

Matt lit a match. It went out.

Matt lit another match. Same thing.

Third time lucky? Not a chance.

Matt looked at Grace.

Grace had a handbag. It was a faux leather cross body with buckle details. Katherine used to own two just like it. It was almost robin egg blue. There was a small tab just inside the main pocket that said the colour was a result of a two-year collaborative process working with a world authority on the colour blue. Jack Eastleigh.

Inside the bag there were shop keys and a lipstick and a

dried-up mascara and a purse full of receipts and a reminder for a dental appointment - with Katherine's husband Clive - and a brochure for the Festival of Sand and a half empty pack of tissues and a nail file and a lip balm and a phone charger cable and a low-fat snack bar wrapper – 'Pumpkin Seed & Prune Surprise' made by Bearing Foods – and a cheap plastic lighter that she didn't even know she had.

Matt tried lighting the edge of the sofa with the lighter. It would be cathartic and liberating. Nothing happened.

He kept trying until the lighter was too hot to hold. It would be a demonstration to the world that he had direction and purpose and ambition and acknowledged the failings of the past. Nothing happened.

Matt looked at Grace.

'It's probably treated with some kind of fire retardant,' she said, tearing pages from 'Elementary Statistics' and screwing them into a ball. She lit the paper with a match and wedged it between the sofa cushions. The fabric caught immediately. Within minutes it was engulfed in a dance of purple and orange flame.

After a while Matt stopped watching the burning sofa and kissed Grace instead.

She was trouble.

cook

Jack stayed at Moss's flat. He didn't do much with his time. He went out and bought beers. He slept on the couch. Every evening he had to cook for a chef. That was the scary part. Moss insisted. She cooked all day. In payment for staying on the couch Jack had to do the cooking. No arguments. No excuses. No premade meals. No hiding the boxes in the bins outside.

Jack was a world authority on the colour blue. He had no great skills with a chopping board. Moss had lots of knives. They were all very sharp. She had lots of ingredients that he had never heard of. None of them were even vaguely blue. She had lots of cookery books that he didn't understand. Her kitchen was the size of a cupboard. The fridge was full of beers. There were a number of obstacles for Jack to overcome. At 8pm he had to put something edible on a plate and watch Moss poke at it with her fork in dismay. It was funny and humiliating and hysterical and mundane. It was just what he needed.

Moss didn't ask questions. Her couch was safe. Moss was a good friend.

Jack always had a shower before he cooked. He would wander around the tiny flat with a towel wrapped around his waist. Moss liked that bit of the cooking best. She wasn't so impressed with his food.

paintbrush

Jack thought about Nadia.

He thought about the panel by Vasco Salvatore Boccamazza entitled '*Virgin in the Garden*' and the Vigo Gualdrini portrait of Theonistus of Milan and the Federigo Badoer portrait and the Cento Ferrazzetta altarpiece and '*The Battle of Cremona de Santa*' and the natural ultramarine pigment that had been made in Venice by the Pio-Padovese family since 1598 – and he felt like a fraud. He did not know blue at all. He was an amateur. He deserved to be deceived.

More beer. More cooking. A stew of beans and root vegetables. Bland and crudely chopped.

Jack thought about Nadia.

He thought about her working in the vault in the basement of a museum in Switzerland. Wearing a magnifying visor with its own illumination. Sitting on a scaffold in front of a hydraulically controlled easel for eight months, repairing an area of damaged canvas that was less than an inch square. It left him feeling stupid and impatient. Of course she was married. He had not seen it because he did not want to. He thought that their shared love of blue was enough.

More beer. More cooking. A rice salad with tinned tuna. Egg noodles with an 'experimental' sweet chili and cumin sauce. Grilled chicken that was still pink inside.

Jack thought about Nadia.

Her family had traded lapis lazuli for more than a thousand years. For a brief moment, she was everything. She was cobalt and cyan and azure and viridian.

But the colour was already beginning to fade. Leak away. It was too intense to last. What they had was now a paintbrush in a jam jar full of cold water. Jack could feel it.

turning

Then something happened. Moss didn't know how it happened. It just did.

Jack made something that actually tasted good.

Moss didn't poke at it with her fork. She didn't pull a face. She was hungry. She cleared her plate. They ate in silence. It was disconcerting. Both of them were shocked. They had a beer. It still didn't make any sense.

Then Jack told Moss about Nadia. Everything. Moss didn't ask questions. She didn't need to. Jack was a world authority on the colour blue. He knew how to tell a story. Then they had another beer.

Then Moss told Jack about Keith. He was her most recent ex-boyfriend. Keith was a bass player in a band that was going nowhere. He lived in a squat that was ten times the size of Moss's flat. Then she found out it wasn't a squat, it was just really untidy. Moss thought that a bass player was a step up from her usual diet of drummers and out-of-work actors, but she was sorely mistaken.

Then they had another beer and laughed at each other. It was funny and humiliating and hysterical and mundane. It was just what they both needed. Then Jack slept on the couch. Moss slept in the room with the bed.

It didn't seem like it, but it was a turning point.

more twit

Daniel didn't know what to make of rolled-up jeans. He hadn't worn rolled-up jeans since he was a child. He wasn't sure he had worn rolled-up jeans even then. They were his father's. He had been there two days and they were already dressing the same. Again.

His father had taken one of the boats from the harbour and gone off to check his lobster pots. He wanted to get to them before the seals or the dolphins did. It made little sense. Daniel was born and brought up in West London. Seals and dolphins were an alien concept to him. His father might as well have said dragons and fairies.

Daniel could hear the small outboard motor chugging away somewhere in the distance. His father was on the other side of a small island in the bay. The island belonged to the house, and the house belonged to his father. And the foreshore. And the mountain behind the house. It was probably not a mountain, but it looked like one to someone who was born and brought up in West London. It was hard to take it all in.

Daniel wasn't sure about the T-shirt either. It was blue and had a picture of a typewriter on it. He still felt like a twit, but in a completely different way.

lobster

Daniel and his father had freshly cooked lobster for lunch with new potatoes dug from a sheltered garden at the side of the house and mayonnaise made with eggs from the hens and a traditional bottle of French white wine that was probably made by someone from Australia.

They sat on a small headland and watched the Kittiwakes and Fulmars and Arctic Turns wheel and tumble above their heads. Daniel's father told him what they were. Daniel thought they were all just seagulls.

'Who was she?' Daniel's father asked.

'I don't really know,' Daniel said.

His father picked up a lobster claw and shook it at him disapprovingly.

'I think you'd better stay for at least a week,' he said.

W

Abby was sitting in a room. It was white. The carpet was white. She was sitting on a white chair. Everything was white. Mrs Haddon was talking. She was talking to two people. One of them was tall. She was wearing a dress. The dress had flowers on it. The flowers were white. The man had eyes that were close together. He didn't have any shoes on. His socks were white. Not as white as the carpet. A different white. Abby didn't say anything. No one was talking to her. Abby knew how to stay quiet. Small. It was easier for her mum.

Mrs Haddon was still talking. She was holding Abby's book. *Galbraith's Boot* Volume 7. It was important somehow. Her grandfather had given it to her. It was written by a witch. That's what he told her. It was about walking somewhere and looking at things and thinking about them. It had pictures of clouds and rivers.

Mrs Haddon stopped talking. The man looked up at the tall lady. Something passed between them that Abby did not understand.

'This is Abigail North,' Mrs Haddon told them.

The tall lady started crying.

witch

David North had several children. He knew the names of some. The first was born when he was twenty-four, the last when he was nearing fifty. He was not what any would call a father. There were three grandchildren – that he was aware of. Abby was the youngest.

David gave his granddaughter the book as a joke. Even as an old man he was cruel. It was the crooked spine of him.

David told Abby that Violet was a witch. He told her that Violet had stolen the family home from them and left them with nothing. He told her that Violet had accomplices. A man with fire for hands and a dog that could change shape and size at will. He told her that Violet had married a ghost who would appear at the doorstep and scratch at the glass to be let in. The ghost was not in possession of a name. He told her that he had tried to recover the great fortune that belonged to the North family but was driven back by Violet and her hideous friends.

Abby could not sleep afterwards. On a mattress on a bare floor in a bare room. It was cold and dark and frightening.

5 things about
Abigail North

Abigail North was a strange, resilient, clever child. She had to be. Her mother had habits. Tics.

Strange sounds wrong. Strange sounds psychological. Odd in some way. She was not. She was different. Ordinary. It's hard to explain. She was a river. She was confronted with an obstacle. She went around it. Over it. No one taught her. It was not circumstance. It was her way.

Resilient sounds wrong. She was not stubborn or thick-skinned or single-minded. She was a mountain or a hill or a stone. She was not a tree in the wind. That much was certain.

Clever sounds cunning and deliberate. She was not that. She was curious and playful. She made a world for herself that was not a mattress on the floor of a bare room. She painted the walls with imaginary flowers and stars and sandcastles and impossible dragons.

The Map of Us

Her mother had habits. Abigail knew that their journey would not be forever. That sounds wrong. But Abigail was right.

falling

Abby's mother fell. It wasn't the first time. It was the last. She did not know that as she fell. How could she? There was little knowing in her falling. That was why she fell. She was not there to hold herself up. She was somewhere behind her eyes and beneath her skin, and her bones were all too big and unruly for her body.

She had fallen before and found herself slumped on the floor in the morning. Or on the stairs. Or by the door. No harm done. This time was different. This time she fell, and she would not get up or wake in clothes bathed in cold sweat or worse. She fell and hit her head on the side of the bath. She did not know that she was in the bathroom. She would never know. She fell.

Her daughter would not see her again. She did not know. Her daughter would find true north. She would be happy there. Happier than she had been in a bare room with bare walls and rules to follow because it was easier for her mother to fall and pick herself up without her daughter looking at her like that.

She fell. And that was an end to falling.

awry

Owen and Violet were married in the village church. The bells did not ring. There was no one there. It was to be expected.

The wedding took place in June, perhaps a year after they met – Violet could not be certain as it had not occurred to her to keep a record at the time. Owen had appeared on her doorstep. She had hoped to be stern and dismissive. It had all gone terribly awry.

Mr Charles S. Juniper gave her away and made a small speech afterwards. Ruth Pennywheal was her bridesmaid. Ruth was a young woman that Mr Juniper had found to proofread Violet's work and make corrections where necessary. She was reliable and efficient and wore Harris tweed skirts, and Mr Juniper was very fond of her.

Violet North retained her name. Owen had no other name to give her. She did not mind. She carried a bouquet of irises and roses from her own large garden. Dog was waiting outside in the wheelbarrow. He would travel to a wedding by no other means.

Mr Juniper and Miss Pennywheal threw confetti and Dog barked as the newlyweds emerged from the church. Then they all walked slowly back to the house at the pace of the bride and laughed and smiled and did not care that the crowd was not bigger or that the bells had not rung.

Arthur Galbraith could not attend. He was busy.

can't

Violet was told that it would be impossible for her to conceive a child. The doctors were wrong.

Violet was told that given the severity of her complications from childhood polio it would be impossible for her to carry her own child to term. The doctors were wrong.

Violet and her baby flourished. She spent long hours in the garden. She grew stronger, not weaker. Owen was always there. So was Dog. He stood guard. He made sure she was not disturbed by dragonflies or beetles or rabbits or any other annoyance. He sometimes dozed in the afternoon sunshine, but he always kept one eye open.

Violet was told that it would endanger her life to continue with the pregnancy that she had already been told was impossible. The doctors were wrong. Violet felt more alive than ever.

Violet was told that it would endanger the life of her unborn child to proceed. That she should consider the convenient thing. Violet decided to be as inconvenient as possible. She did a grand job.

Violet gave birth in her own home without complication.

267

Jules Preston

Her daughter was healthy and vocal and of a good weight. Such are impossible things.

Owen and Mr Juniper were in the next room. Mr Juniper shook Owen's hand. Mr Juniper was wearing gloves as he always did. Owen understood the significance of the gesture and hugged his friend heartily and did a little jig that Mr Juniper tried to replicate as best he could. Mr Juniper could not dance, but he danced that night.

Dog left them and found his place under the desk in Violet's study. He slept most soundly until morning.

defined

Our lives are defined by volumes of *Galbraith's Boot*.

My mother was born between 'Walks from Blind Holt to Pin Common' and 'Walks from Haresfoot Levels to Hanger's Pit.' Owen and Violet called her Rose. It was her name.

Rose North would sit on Violet's lap while she typed or ride around the garden in a wheelbarrow pushed by her father or play with a dog called 'Dog.' We all did the same when it was our time. Except me. I was too young.

When my mother married my father, the tradition continued.

Katherine was born 19 miles into Volume 8: 'Walks from Broom Marsh to New Mountsley Yard.'

Jack was born towards the end of Volume 10: 'Walks from Mill Cott Lane to Peddler's Oven.'

I was born during the preparatory notes and sketches for Volume 11: 'Walks from Sweet Hill to Brown Loaf Steps.'

We have all been part of Arthur's adventures on the Great Moor. Except me. I was too young.

It explains a lot.

5 things about Owen

Owen was not always a gardener. Before he was a gardener he was the sound of a bumblebee clambering inside a foxglove flower. Or the smell of a garden after the rain has stopped. Or the first bite of an apple picked from the tree that is sour and sweet and not yet stored but is delicious all the same. Or the dance of a blackbird or the stare of a fox. He was outside, not inside. He was a wheelbarrow and a dog and a spade, not a locked door or a closed window or a drawn curtain. He was a breath. A cool breeze that would travel as far again simply to move a strand of her hair.

Owen was tall and spare and gentle and persuasive. He did not *make* things grow. He asked for their help. Not all agreed. That was the way of things. He accepted that. He would ask more gently next time.

Owen lived by the clock of dusk and dawn and paid no attention to minutes and hours. He did not own a watch or covet the keeping of one. His sleeves were always rolled. His hands were always muddy. He had fingers for a comb and a water butt to dip his head and a sharp pruning knife on his belt that would cut as well at midnight as at noon.

Owen knew how to coax a fire and dissuade a snail.

Owen pushed his daughter around the garden in a wheelbarrow from near the moment she was born. She was a queen. The dog that had been king did not mind. He ran beside them and barked and jumped and tried to impress her and would let no harm come to her even if she tugged his tail or pulled his ears or fell asleep on him under the shade of the apple tree. He would not move until she was awake again.

the proposal

Mr Juniper wrote a letter. It was difficult for him to hold a pen. Uncomfortable. More than that. He did not complain. He persevered.

He wrote it when the offices of Twelvetrees, Juniper and Brompton were quiet. Early in the morning, or late into the evening when his father and Mr Brompton had gone home.

He tried many pens and finally settled on one with a double broad nib and blue ink that he found in the corner room formally occupied by the late Mr Twelvetrees. He had been gone for some time, but his room was still much as he left it. He had a fine selection of pens that he no longer needed. Still, Mr Juniper would put it back when he finished.

Mr Juniper wanted the letter to be full of love, to be open and honest and hide nothing, but each word was a hardship for him. His hands would not allow it. His hands protested. After three days he had to stop. A few days later he tried again. His hands were worse than before. He persisted.

He ignored his thumb. It was the worst culprit by far. Instead, he held the pen slotted between his middle and index finger. That was better. The letter inched forward.

After two weeks it was done.

It was not all that he had hoped for, but he could go no further with it.

'Marry me,' it said.

He gave the letter to Ruth Pennywheal.

Ruth Pennywheal's
reply

Dear Sidney

Thank you for your letter. I am sorry that I cannot accept your most unexpected offer of marriage.

Please do not think of me as shallow or uncaring. I am not. At least I do not think I am. I will let you be the judge of that.

I have worked for your father at the offices of Twelvetrees, Juniper and Brompton on the third floor of 14a Sneed Street, London for the last eight years and know you to be a kind and generous man – if sometimes a little secretive. You have a magnificent moustache.

I am, of course, grateful for the opportunity of working with Mrs North and her wonderful books.

I simply cannot find it in my heart to accept a proposal from a man who wears gloves all the time. I hope you understand.

With kind regards
Ruth Pennywheal (Miss)

drawer

I was sorting through the drawer under the coffee table in the hallway. The coffee table was in the hallway because it was long and feeble and not much use for coffee cups or bowls of soup or bottles of wine or anything else that you didn't want to topple onto the carpet every time you tiptoed past it.

I had some heavy-duty black bin liners left over from packing up the last of Matt's stuff. I thought that I'd put them to good use and tidy up a little. The drawer under the coffee table wouldn't close properly anymore. It seemed as if everything got swept into it and forgotten.

I opened the drawer. The entire table wobbled on its flimsy legs.

The top layer was mostly renewal forms for the Pilates classes at the local leisure centre that I only went to once. And the tai-chi classes and the yoga classes and the reminder that I hadn't been to aqua fit in three months and my membership was about to run out. I put those straight in the bag.

Beneath was a rich seam of junk mail addressed only to 'The Occupier.' Apparently these were definitely not circulars but contained important documents and should be opened immediately. I opened one. It was a brochure for loft insulation. I put all of those in the bag, too.

I found the crumpled envelope that Matt's mother gave us as a wedding gift. The IOU written on the back of a shopping list was still inside. I decided not to give the envelope back. I threw it in the bag with all the other junk.

At the bottom of the drawer – under a dead spider, a 3amp fuse and a foil sachet of paracetamol caplets with all the pills popped out – I found a bundle of photocopied pages from *Galbraith's Boot* stapled together. My mother had typed them. They were her first attempt to replicate the work of my grandmother. They were typed on the same turquoise blue Royal Quiet Deluxe typewriter that she had used. I could tell. I could see where the 'e' had got stuck. They were corrected in pencil in my mother's familiar handwriting. I remember her sending me the pages. She wanted my honest opinion. I was too busy to read them at the time. I was crunching the numbers on some low-fat cereal bar or other. I put her work in the drawer underneath the rickety coffee table that was exiled in the hallway and promptly forgot all about them.

5 things about my mother

My mother had two lefts. She was the navigator. It was a drawback. Any journey with my mother would probably take somewhat longer than expected.

'Turn left at the roundabout,' my mother would say. The map would be crumpled in her lap like a bag of chips. Three hours earlier it would have been new. She always tortured maps that way. On the way home she would flatten them out by sitting on them.

My father would turn left at the roundabout.

'Not that left!' My mother would shriek. 'The other left!'

My father would say nothing. He would drum his fingers on the steering wheel for a moment and then find a safe place to turn the car around. It would be an old estate car. French. Full of sand. The three of us in the back.

The first time I took my driving test I ended up in the resident's car park behind a block of flats. I blame my mother.

My mother was the daughter of a woman who could not walk far and a man who had only one name. She had grown up in a house of pure wonder. Her company as a child was a dog called 'Dog' that was many different dogs of the same name and the inhabitants of a large garden. She kept treasures. Small things. Feathers. Leaves. She said 'hello' to butterflies. Always. She took nothing for granted.

My mother let Katherine wear dresses and Jack decorate himself and me play with numbers. She had two lefts. She was confident that we would find our own way. We did.

My mother wrote four volumes of *Galbraith's Boot*. She left a fifth unfinished. Volume 17: 'Walks from Rook's Wood to Coldbank Ruins.' She did not mean to leave it unfinished. She had cancer.

My mother died a year before Matt and I split up. She was fifty-two.

October

I was there when she left us. For the quiet moments before and after. She was holding my hand, and then she was not. She was no longer in the room.

My father had gone home to sleep for a few hours. My sister was not due to return until the following day. My brother never appeared at the hospice at all. It was his way of coping. It was just me. I didn't know what to do next. Who to tell. What would happen. I didn't want to leave her alone even though I knew she was somewhere else and wouldn't mind. I felt protective and forlorn and something else that I couldn't quite place. Cheated.

She was fifty-two in March. We had sponge cake filled with homemade rhubarb jam and egg and cress sandwiches with the crusts cut off and drank tall glasses of sloe gin and lemonade until well after midnight. Now it was October. March seemed like a lifetime ago.

I wondered whether I should collect the cards from her bedside table and take them with me. And the flowers. Or did someone else do that? I sat beside her for a moment and said goodbye softly but out loud. Then I went and found a nurse.

The staff were comforting and polite and went about the business of a departure without urgency or fuss. I waited outside. I called my father. He did not need me to tell him what had happened. I called my sister. She would not be returning the next day after all. I called my brother and left a message. He refused to answer the phone directly. It was his way of coping. I called Matt. He said it was for the best.

I didn't see my mother again. I imagined her sitting in the front seat of an old estate car with a map crumpled in her lap like a bag of chips at the beginning of new adventure that would probably take somewhat longer than expected.

'Turn left at the next roundabout,' she would say. 'No, the other left!'

I miss her. We all do.

tide

Hard to get to.
Park the car.
Walk.
No other way.
Through a field.
Join a path.
Tunnel of hawthorn and blackthorn.
Turns steeply downwards.
Back on itself.
Again and again.
Down.
Keep going.
Don't lose hope.
Just a trowel
and the wooden handle of a spoon and a brush.
Take nothing else.
I'm sorry I was not there.
I am so sorry.
An hour.
Perhaps less.

Jules Preston

Will find it.
Just below.
A small cove.
Empty.
Hard to get to.
Few people know.
Round stones
and jagged brown slate
standing upwards.
And sand.
Red.
And plastic bottles
and rope
and wood worn smooth
and a small stream dividing the beach
heading for the comfort of the sea.
Sit a while.
Gather what thoughts you have.
You will not be disturbed.
Not here.
I'm sorry I was not there.
I am so sorry.
Take a trowel
and the wooden handle of a spoon
and a brush
and start at one end.
In the sun if you must.
A handful of sand is enough.
Make a mound.

The Map of Us

Cut petals with the trowel.
Curl the edges with the handle of the spoon.
Soften them with the brush
and repeat until you are in the sun no more.
Draw leaves and stems
until the beach is a hundred roses.
Then write her name in the sand
and wait
and watch
for the tide to come
and take her from you again.
I'm sorry I was not there.
I am so sorry.

blub

There has been a steady increase in tears over the last few days. It caught me by surprise. I thought I had done all my crying, but I seem to have encountered a stubborn patch of secondary welling up and flooding that has me shaking my head and laughing at myself all at the same time.

Packet tissues are a waste of time. I have to carry a toilet roll with me wherever I go. I have others positioned in strategic locations around the flat. There is one in the bathroom. Obviously. And one on the floor of the living room where the sofa used to be. I have two more in the bedroom – just in case I have a sudden downpour and need the extra absorbency.

I don't even know what I'm crying about. Mum? Matt? Bailey? Seedy-Pea-Nut-Slices? 10.37am?

Just thinking about it makes me start to blub. What's going on? I'm a wreck.

swim

10.37am? It was a conference. After a conference. The morning after. I wasn't staying in the same hotel as everyone else. I was on my own in another hotel. Some sort of mix up. It was a much better hotel than the hotel I was supposed to be staying in. It had a gym and a heated indoor swimming pool.

Trish and Helen were staying in the hotel they were supposed to be staying in. Their booking didn't get mixed up like mine. Their hotel didn't have a gym or a swimming pool though. They got free newspapers and an ironing board in their room.

The conference was about healthy snacks and smoothies. It was held annually. They called it the 'Healthy Snacks & Smoothies Annual Conference.' There were workshops and keynote speakers and breakout sessions in the afternoon and an award ceremony at the end. Everyone involved in the healthy snacks and smoothies market was there. Bearing Foods won two awards. I don't know what for. I wasn't there. I'd already gone back to my hotel.

I go to the conference every year. I have to go. Compass Applied Analytics picks up a lot of work from attending. Helen and Trish love it. I'd rather wax my armpits.

I dumped my dreary 'welcome pack' and ghastly 'goody bag' in my room and went off to find the swimming pool. I bought a swimming costume in the spa shop next to the gym and got changed.

The pool was long and thin. The room had a vaulted glass ceiling and was lit like a spaceship. There were wooden loungers around the sides. The pool was empty.

I didn't dive in. I thought about it. First I checked the temperature of the water with my toe. It was warm. I sat on the edge and slowly slid into the water. It was utterly delicious. I pushed off from the wall and felt a day of talking and listening and pretending to make notes and yawning and wondering when the next coffee break would be simply dissolve away. I turned over onto my back and looked up through the glass ceiling. It was getting dark. The moon was out. I could see stars. I could see planes coming in to land at the nearby international airport. I started kicking my feet and splashing my arms like an excited child.

I didn't realise that I was being watched.

him

I got to the end of the pool and turned around to come back in the opposite direction. That's when I saw him. He was lying on one of the loungers. I'm not sure why I hadn't noticed him before. I was probably too busy making a fool of myself.

He was wearing a grey suit. A white shirt. Black shoes and grey socks. He was dripping. He was soaking wet. He must have been swimming with his clothes on. I could see the trail of water from the edge of the pool to the lounger. He wasn't really looking at me. He glanced in my direction and then looked away again. I knew who it was.

Daniel Bearing.

deep end

I couldn't just ignore him. I tried to stand up. I couldn't. I was in the deep end. It wasn't very deep, but it was still deeper than me. I swam to the edge of the pool.

'Are you okay?' I said.

It was a stupid question, but it was the best that I could do given the circumstances. I was in a swimming costume that didn't quite fit in the swimming pool of a hotel that I wasn't supposed to be staying in talking to the owner of one of the biggest companies in low-fat snack bars who had just taken a dip in his suit.

He looked at me.

'I'm tired,' he said.

Then he got up and dived back into the pool. His shoe came off. It floated to the surface and bobbed aimlessly in front of me.

He was under the water for a long time. A very long time. I was about to hold my breath and see where he had got to. Then he came up for air.

I handed him his shoe.

'Sorry,' he said. 'It's been a long day.'

I nodded.

'Do you want to get something to eat?' he said.

I nodded. I was hungry.

reservations

Of course it sounds strange now. It was pretty strange then. I had just been asked to dinner in the deep end of a hotel swimming pool by a man in a suit with a shoe in his hand. That sort of thing doesn't happen very often. Not to me anyway.

Daniel got out of the pool and started to undress. He took off his remaining shoe. Then his socks. Then his suit jacket. His tie, then shirt. Lastly his trousers. They clung to his legs. He had to hop about to get them off. He got them off. He was wearing boxer shorts. They had puffins on them. He left his wet clothes in a pile on the poolside.

I watched the whole thing. I was treading water. My legs ached, and I could hardly breath by the time he disappeared into the changing room. I didn't know where we were going to eat. Or what time. He didn't say.

whisk

Moss was on her way home. Jack was cooking. She didn't know what he was cooking, but it was going to be good. He was experimenting with brown rice and green lentils. It sounded plain and stodgy. It wasn't. Moss picked up the pace. Jack still took a shower every night before cooking. If she didn't stop to buy beers she might make it back in time to catch him with a towel around his waist. And wet hair. And rivulets of water running down his back. Moss thought about buying some trainers so she could jog home. Then she remembered. She had tried jogging once. Hated it. Threw up in a bush. In someone's front garden. They were in the garden at the time. Pruning a pink and purple hydrangea. The bush she was throwing up in. It was beyond embarrassing. She knew them. They ate in the restaurant. They hadn't booked a table in a while.

Moss had met Nadia. Not exactly met. She was in the restaurant for lunch. Moss saw the booking. 1.30pm. Danti. Table for two. She came with her husband. Moss assumed it was her husband. It could have been someone else. Nadia didn't look like a world authority on the colour blue either.

She looked like someone who had met Jack on a plane and whisked him straight off to bed.

The same thought had crossed Moss's mind too. Forgetting the plane part. And the whisking. There wouldn't be much whisking in Moss's flat. It was way too small to whisk. Maybe some gentle nudging. Yeah. Nudging might work.

Moss didn't want to spoil anything. Jack had been a friend for years. Despite being a world authority on the colour blue, he was normal and easy-going and good company and funny and disarming and fallible. He wasn't a drummer or a bass player or an out-of-work actor. They were the worst.

If he was still in a towel by the time she got home, she might have to nudge. Gently. Test the water. Rivulets of water running down his back. Wet hair. She thought about buying trainers again. She started to trot.

decision

'She missed a bit,' Grace said. She was naked.

'Who missed a bit?' Matt said. He was naked, too.

'Tilly,' Grace said.

They weren't doing anything. They were both just naked. It was Grace's idea. She wanted to see what she was getting herself into before she made any firm decision about doing anything. She was taking her time, too.

'What bit?' Matt said.

'The Compatibility Index,' Grace said. 'It's supposed to be the centrepiece of the report, but it's not here.'

'So?' Matt said.

At first he found the close scrutiny a little unsettling, but he was getting used to it now. It had never occurred to him that Grace would have freckles all over. She was trouble.

'I'd like to see it. Wouldn't you?' Grace said.

'I'll call her tomorrow,' Matt said.

'Try not to hang up,' Grace said.

Grace had seen the 'Hanging Up' graph. It was on Page 18 of the report. Matt did a lot of hanging up. Maybe not as bad

293

as his 'Three-Seater Sofa Usage,' but it was still a pretty significant amount of unnecessary hanging up.

'I won't hang up,' Matt said.

'Good,' Grace said.

Then they stopped talking and did something. Grace had made her mind up.

Four hours later, when Matt had finally got his breath back, he had to admit that she made the right decision.

glass

Matt rang Tilly the next day.

'Hi Tilly. It's Matt,' he said.

'If you're just going to hang up on me again, I'm not interested,' Tilly said flatly.

'I'm not going to hang up on you,' Matt said.

'Okay. As long as you're sure you're not going to hang up on me,' Tilly said.

'I'm sure,' Matt said.

'Oh,' Tilly said. She was surprised. She was expecting a lot more hanging up.

'Grace wants to know if you can send us a copy of the Compatibility Index,' Matt said.

There was a silence. Not an awkward silence or an angry silence. An intrigued silence.

'Who is Grace?' Tilly said.

'She's great,' Matt said.

'That wasn't what I asked,' Tilly said, pointedly.

'By the way, I thought the "Sexual Activity" graph was a bit harsh,' Matt said. 'But Grace thinks it was the "Three-Seater Sofa Usage" that highlighted the real issues.'

There was another silence. This one was a different kind of silence again. It was an utterly incredulous silence with steep glass walls and nothing for Tilly's words to hold onto. 'Do you know anything about freckles?' Matt said.

NW

Abby woke up in the white house. She had her own bed. She got up and put her school uniform on. She wasn't going to school. School was hours away. It was all she had. She went downstairs.

Clive was in the kitchen. He was her uncle. He wasn't really. He was something else. It was hard to explain. Mrs Haddon had tried. Then she left. It was late. She had a long drive back.

The kitchen was mostly white, but there was red paint on the wall. And green paint, and orange. And colours all mixed together. There was paint on the floor. And splashes of paint on the window. Whoever did the painting didn't know how to paint. They needed painting lessons.

'Morning, Abby,' Clive said. He was eating toast.

Abby didn't say anything.

'What do you want for breakfast?'

Abby had never been asked that before. She just got her own. Always. It was easier for her mum.

'Toast?' Clive said.

Abby didn't say anything.

Clive put two pieces of bread in the toaster anyway.

Abby stood in the doorway. She didn't know where to go. She didn't know if she was allowed to sit down. She didn't know the rules. Mum had rules. It was easier that way.

cake

The dog came across Mr Juniper in the garden. He was pleased to see him. He barked. It was a welcoming bark, not a warning. Mr Juniper was always welcome. Mr Juniper often had a piece of sandwich in his pocket. Or a corner of cake, or half a biscuit. Today it was cake. It was fresh cake, not dry, old, stale-tasting cake. There was lemon in the cake. He could smell it. Lemon cake was not the dog's favourite kind of cake, but it was fresh cake, and it was being offered to him. It would be churlish to refuse. He took it gently and then followed Mr Juniper deeper into the garden hoping that there might be another bit of cake still in his pocket. He would have followed him even if there wasn't.

Mr Juniper did not know the large garden as the dog did, and soon their roles were reversed and the dog was leading the way. It was right and proper. The dog was a king. Except when cake was involved. Or half a biscuit.

The dog lead Mr Juniper directly to Owen, then saw something in the bushes that required his immediate attention and left them alone together.

found

Mr Juniper handed Owen an envelope. It was sealed and did not seem to hold much. Certainly no more than a single sheet of paper.

'What is it? Owen asked, holding it up to the sun.

'It is your name,' Mr Juniper said. 'The other one. The one that was thought to be lost.'

Owen looked more closely at the envelope.

'How did you find it?'

'I went looking,' Mr Juniper said. 'I thought that you might like it to be returned.'

Owen smiled.

'Thank you,' he said.

'It is my very great pleasure,' Mr Juniper said.

'Is it a good name?' Owen asked, full of concern.

Mr Juniper shook his head.

'I have no idea. I asked the person who said they knew it to write it down and then place it in this envelope. They gave it to me much as I have just given it to you. That is the sum total of my involvement in the matter.'

'Should I open it?' Owen said.

'That is not for me to say. It's up to you.'

'What shall I do with it then?' Owen asked.

'Anything you wish,' Mr Juniper said, turning to go into the house. 'It is your name, not mine.'

lost again

Hours passed. Days. Owen did not open the envelope.

Weeks. Months. He kept it in his pocket and did not think of it. He never spoke of its existence to his wife. He knew that Mr Juniper would not mention it.

A year went by. He thought of it then. It was enough time to reach a decision. He put it on the fire unopened. It did not matter.

The timing of rain mattered.

The angle of the sun mattered.

The warmth of the soil mattered.

The quality of seed mattered.

The edge of a spade mattered.

The shade of a tree mattered.

His name did not.

He had come this far without it.

It was a generous gift from a friend.

That mattered. That was all that mattered.

The envelope curled and caught, and for a moment the name was visible, and then it was an ember.

The Map of Us

Some things were better lost.
There was no going back.
Mr Juniper would understand.

wish

I found Daniel Bearing in the hotel restaurant at 7pm. It was a guess. He had not been there long. He was wearing a grey suit, black tie and a white shirt. This time he wasn't soaking wet. I sat down.

He looked at me.

I looked at him.

Silence.

Great start.

I was hungry.

I should have ordered room service.

'Matilda,' he said finally.

It seems I was wrong again. Daniel Bearing called me Matilda, too.

'Yes,' I said. 'Daniel.'

'Yes,' he said.

This was going well.

I looked at the menu.

He looked at the menu.

He sipped his drink.

I wanted a drink.

As if by magic, a waiter appeared.

'May I get you something to drink?' he asked.

See? Magic.

'Yes, I'll have whatever he's having,' I said, nodding towards Daniel.

The waiter barely raised an eyebrow.

'Another tap water? Of course.'

He disappeared.

Good waiter, I thought.

I looked at the menu again.

Daniel sipped his drink.

'Compass Applied Analytics?' Daniel said.

'Yes,' I said.

Daniel made a sound that I didn't quite catch. A sort of desolate sigh with a growl mixed in somewhere at the back of his throat. Charming.

'Bearing Foods,' I said, not wanting to be outdone.

'Yes,' he said.

I made a sound that didn't come out quite right. I was hoping for something barely audible and enigmatic, but it ended up being really loud and rather horsey.

'Oh,' he said.

I wished I had stayed in my room.

I wished I had stayed at the conference.

I wished I hadn't come back early and gone swimming.

I wished I had left him dripping on his lounger and not said a thing and tried to creep out of the pool without catching his eye.

I wished.

'Why did you leave the conference early?' he said.
None of my wishes came true.

broken

My drink arrived.

Tap water.

No ice.

Yeah.

Great.

Bloody conferences.

Bloody hotels.

Bloody swimming pools.

Bloody snack bars.

Bloody numbers.

Bloody Daniel Bearing.

'Thanks,' I said to the waiter. I smiled. He turned his back and walked off.

'My father lives in the Outer Hebrides now,' Daniel said.

There were so many words strung together in a sentence that it took me a moment to work out what they all meant.

'Does he?' I said. I was going to say something else, but I ran out of the energy required to live, so I didn't bother.

'Yes,' he said. 'I'm having the mushroom tagliatelle. What are you going to have?' He said.

I didn't answer him. There was something strange happening with the lights.

There was a light directly behind him. Not bright or in my eyes. Just there. Right behind him. I moved my head from side to side. I could see tiny points of light. I could see through him. He was full of cracks. He was all broken.

I was hungrier than I thought. I sipped my water. It was tepid. I ordered bread and olives and tomato and basil soup and linguini with capers and chili and a green salad and a large glass of frosty white wine.

I tried not to look at the lights. They were sad and kind of pretty.

truth

Our food turned up. Daniel had a tiny bowl of mushroom tagliatelle. There was probably a mushroom hiding in there somewhere, but no more than one. I had a basin of soup and half a loaf of bread and a whole jar of marinated olives and a huge bowl of linguine and a plate piled high with salad leaves and a humungous glass of chilled white wine.

Daniel glanced across the table.

'You didn't answer my question,' he said.

Which one? I thought.

'Why did you leave the conference early?'

Oh. That one.

I took a sip of my wine. It was cold and dry and exhilarating, and I decided to eat something before I had any more. Now was no time for honesty.

I was honest.

'I was bored,' I said. 'I was bored of yoghurt covered snack bars and goji berries and puffed brown rice and the endless arguments about chocolate chips and the digestive properties of coconut. It's always the same. I hate coming to these stupid conferences.'

309

I stopped myself.

Daniel looked at me.

I looked at Daniel.

Whoops. I thought.

'Do you want to know the truth?' he said.

'Yes,' I said. Because why not? Now was no time for something vague and meaningless.

'So do I,' he said.

He was smiling.

He had a nice smile.

It was the first time I'd seen it. It changed him.

'Help yourself to bread,' I said

'Thanks,' he said.

He helped himself to bread.

'And salad,' I said.

'Thanks,' he said.

He helped himself to salad.

'Would you like a glass of wine?' I said.

'Thanks,' he said.

I called the waiter over and ordered a bottle.

The waiter seemed happier, too.

when

We ate. We talked. We drank a bottle of wine. Then another.
Nothing happened.

We ordered ice cream. I had vanilla. He had chocolate. I
let him have a spoon of mine. He wouldn't let me have a
spoon of his. He fended off my spoon. We had a spoon fight.
I won. He didn't let me win or anything. It was a fair fight. I
took a big spoon of his ice cream. It was good ice cream.

Nothing happened.

We didn't have coffees. We argued about who was paying
the bill. It was a good argument. He brought up a High Court
case from 1812. I went with moral outrage. In the end he held
a salt shaker behind his back. I had to guess. I picked the
right hand. It was in the right hand. He changed the rules
and paid the bill.

Nothing happened.

We said goodnight and went our separate ways.

Nothing happened.

It was the following morning. I was on my way to the hotel
reception to check out. I met Daniel in the corridor.

That's when it happened.

10.37am happened then.
It's all in the flow chart.
Page 5.
It's all there.

eventually

Jack had promised to go and see an old friend of his grand-mother. He asked Moss if she'd like to come along. Moss said okay. If Jack wasn't going to have a shower and walk around the flat with a towel wrapped around his waist and then cook something, there wasn't much point staying in on her own.

They walked through the park, past the playground with the swings and the tall slide and the not-so-tall slide and the sandpit where Jack's father learned everything he needed to know.

The cafe was closed. Predictably. There were half a dozen pigeons sunning themselves on the roof.

Some things don't change.

Most things do.

Eventually.

mistake

Ruth Pennywheal greeted them at the door. She was in her late eighties. She was wearing a hacking jacket and a Harris tweed skirt and a pair of orthopaedic slippers. She gave Jack a robust and lengthy hug. She had to reach up. Then she looked at Moss. She was uncertain for a moment. Then she gave Moss a lengthy and robust hug as well. Ruth didn't have many visitors. She saw an opportunity for a hug and she took it.

Ruth's flat was even smaller than Moss's. It was one room on the ground floor. It was dark and stuffy. The windows had bars on them. The stairs to the flats above cut a diagonal across one wall. There was a waste pipe in the corner covered over with wallpaper. Not the same wallpaper. Different wallpaper. There were only two chairs. Moss sat on the floor. The carpet was thin and covered in a thick layer of grey dust. It was another colour underneath.

'How is Mr Juniper?' Ruth asked.

'Sidney is fine,' Jack said. 'He stays at the house most of the time. He has trouble remembering things. He can't say much. He likes the garden.'

Ruth seemed lost in thought for a moment. She looked around the dark stuffy room with the bars on the windows as if she was seeing it for the first time. Somebody flushed a toilet upstairs. Water and whatever else rushed down the waste pipe in the corner. Ruth looked at Moss.

'You like Jack, don't you?' She said.

'Yes,' Moss said.

'Grab him then and hold on tight,' Ruth said. 'Don't make the same mistake that I did.'

soon

Jack and Moss walked back through the park.

Jack was telling Moss about Violet and Arthur Galbraith and the sixteen volumes of *Galbraith's Boot* and the turquoise blue Royal Quiet Deluxe typewriter and the study that was turned into a painted map and the North family and Mr Charles S. Juniper and how he once proposed to Ruth Pennywheal by letter and she turned him down because he wore gloves.

Moss listened. Jack didn't notice when she took his hand. He was talking about people that he loved. More than the colour blue. More than anything. She hoped that he might feel the same way about her. If not now. Soon.

score

Trish was waiting for me in my office. She was sitting in my chair. She looked different. She was wearing pumps and a cashmere tunic dress and a loosely knotted scarf. She had a copy of my Compatibility Index in her hand. She didn't seem to have a wasp in her ear. It had gone. Flown away. She was smiling. I wasn't sure if I was in trouble or not.

'Am I in trouble?' I asked, more out of habit really.

'No,' Trish said. 'I wanted to thank you in person.'

Now I was even more confused.

There was a number written on the front of the Index. '93.' It had a series of question marks and exclamations after it. The whole thing was circled in pen. It was just ordinary pen, but it was hard to miss.

'Helen found your questionnaire by the printer,' Trish said. 'She gave me a copy.'

'By the printer' was an interesting way of putting it. Helen had stolen it.

'Where is Helen?' I said.

'She's taking a few days off. She's trying to track down her

317

first husband. Their marriage may have only lasted for nine days, but they have a lot to talk about. He scored 85.'

delirious

It seems we were all wrong. The reason for Trish's look of peeved intolerance wasn't botched plastic surgery or inflamed unmentionables or a wasp jammed in her ear – it was insecurity. She wasn't sure about her husband.

My Compatibility Index had changed all that. She had filled it in fearing the worst. She expected a score in the low 50s, maybe even the high 40s. He scored 93%. When he got home that night, she pounced on him. She was deliriously happy. She proved it to him on the stairs. And again on the kitchen table. And yet again on the floor in the lounge. She was going to have to do something about the stripped pine floorboards. One hundred and twenty questions had changed her life.

Trish left my office and went straight to the kitchenette. She took down her policy directive about smiling in the workplace and tore it into lots of very small pieces. Then she had a little cry all to herself. Just a little one. Then she tottered off towards the toilets. I guess wearing flat-soled shoes takes a bit of getting used to.

toast

Abby ate the toast as quietly as she could. She made sure that all the crumbs went on the plate. It was good toast. Clive watched her eat it. He ate toast, too. When they had finished, he put two more slices of bread in the toaster. Abby didn't mind. It was good toast. Clive didn't say anything about more toast. He didn't say anything about anything. Abby didn't say anything either. They just ate toast.

Katherine came into the kitchen.

She was Abby's aunt.

She wasn't really.

She sat down across the table.

Abby ate toast.

'I can cancel today's appointments,' Clive said.

'We'll be fine,' Katherine said.

'Better let your father know what's happened. And Tilly.'

'I'll do it later.'

Abby ate toast. She wondered who Tilly was.

Clive got up and put his plate in the sink.

'Nice toast,' Abby said.

'So that's what you sound like,' Clive said. Then he left the room.

Abby liked him already.

not Katherine

I was hiding in my office. It has glass walls. Maybe 'hiding' was the wrong word? Everyone wanted a copy of the Compatibility Index. I was keeping my head down hoping that no one would notice me. My phone rang. I answered it immediately. Even with the door closed it was making a noise. I didn't want to draw attention to myself.

'Tilly?'

Katherine. My sister. Never called me at work. Never. Not Katherine.

'Yeah?'

'Where's dad?' she said.

Katherine never calls him dad. Never. Not Katherine.

'I don't know,' I said.

'He's not at home. I tried.'

'A beach somewhere?' I said.

'Where?'

'I'll find out.'

'Can you call me back?'

'What's wrong?'

'Nothing. I need to see dad,' she said.

'Okay. Give me five minutes.'

'Thanks,' she said.

Katherine never said thanks. Never. Not Katherine.

Something had happened. The world was shifting. I could tell.

perfect

Wrong hat.
South westerly.
Backing south.
Gusty.
Unpredictable.
Change in the weather.
Wrong hat.
Car full of hats.
Straw.
All the same.
Different sizes.
Need a tight hat.
Not a medium tight hat.
Not a sunhat.
Not a still-warm-day hat.
Need a south-westerly-backing-south-gusty-change-in-the-weather hat.
Idiot.
Picked the wrong hat.
What was I thinking?

The Map of Us

Any minute now.
Watch it fly off.
Roll away.
Miles down the beach.
Too old to run after it.
Can't run in sandals.
Everyone laughing.
Already behind.
Stupid dragon.
Bloody nose.
Snout.
Muzzle.
Whatever.
Try again.
Do it right.
Haven't got time for the wrong hat.
Idiot.
Look up.
Catch sight of something.
Mirage.
Sand blowing in my eyes.
Wrong hat doesn't help.
Stand up.
See better then.
Above the sand blowing.
Take my hat off.
Katherine.
Coming towards me.
Shoes in her hand.

Must be.
Katherine.
Someone with her.
A child.
A girl.
A mystery.
Sand in my eyes.
No.
Not a mystery.
She's a North.
I can tell she's a North.
Katherine.
In my arms.
Crying.
Dad.
Dad.
Dad.
Never calls me dad.
Never.
Not Katherine.
Hold her.
She holds me.
Everything stops.

Then starts again.
Child smiles.
Points.
'Dragon,' she says.
'Yes.'

The Map of Us

'Can I help?' she says.
'Yes.'
Three of us.
Together.
Later we have ice cream.
Perfect.

tick tick tick

Grace was flicking through the Compatibility Index. She stopped and looked at her watch.

'Fourteen minutes,' she said.

'Is that all?' Matt said.

Matt was naked again. Grace wasn't. She was seeing how long he could take it.

'It's a great questionnaire,' Grace said. 'It's comprehensive, focused, well balanced and accessible. We could do something with a questionnaire like that.'

'Like what?' Matt said

'Compatibility consultations,' Grace said. 'Everybody wants a number. A simple diagram. Something they can understand at a glance. You could ask all the same questions. Just use the present tense for new relationships and the past tense for post mortems on failed marriages like yours.'

'Thanks.' Matt said, darkly.

'Fourteen minutes thirty seconds,' Grace said.

'What if you get it wrong?' Matt said.

'It doesn't matter. It's a signpost. An indication. That's all.'

Matt was trying hard to hide an indication of his own.

'Numbers are a poor measure of love,' Grace said wistfully.

'Deep,' Matt said.

'It's a quote,' Grace said. 'Millicent Fenwick. She's a mathematician. She theorised that love was a paradox that eluded standard and nonstandard notions of equivalence and analysis.'

Matt put his hands on his naked hips. 'How do you know that?' he said.

'She's my mum,' Grace said, looking at her watch again. 'Fifteen minutes.'

Matt sighed.

'You're going to ask Tilly if we can use it,' Grace said.

'Why do I have to ask?' Matt said.

Grace slowly unbuttoned her shirt. One button. Two. She wasn't wearing a bra. Matt could see the freckled skin between her breasts. For a moment her hand hovered over the third button. The only thing that was holding her shirt together. Then she took her hand away.

'Because,' she said.

Matt was having difficulty concentrating.

Yeah. She was trouble alright.

5 things about Daniel's father

Daniel's father lived in a former shooting lodge in the Outer Hebrides that had its own stone harbour and a beach of pure white sand and nine bedrooms and views to the Isle of Skye. He had worked for twelve hours a day, six days a week for over thirty years to build Bearing Foods into an award-winning company with an annual turnover in the millions. Then he retired to a bare, windswept headland in the North Atlantic in search of something else. He did not know what. He would find out when he got there.

Daniel's father had hair implants. It was a bit of a culture shock.

Daniel's father stood on the harbour wall as the sun dipped and looked out across a troubled sea. He drank wine and wondered what he would do next. He bought walking boots. They did not fit. He exchanged them for walking boots that did fit and set about exploring his new home. He was in no hurry.

He felt as if he had been taken back in time somehow. It was a curious feeling to be so removed – so distant and yet not alone. He carried a notebook so that he could sketch the places that he had been. He could not draw well.
Sometimes he despaired and went home. It came upon him suddenly. He could not say why. He had to learn to walk more slowly. He was still dancing in time to a life he had left behind.

Daniel's father began to recognise the dark shapes of mountains on the distant horizon. He traveled further every day. He felt set adrift. Free. The land seemed to stretch away forever. He hoped to know it all one day. He found that he was busier than he had ever been.

Daniel's father decided to have his hair cut short. Hair implants had no place in the North Atlantic.
His son arrived the same day. He was due to stay a week. He didn't. A week was not enough. He stayed for much longer.

sore feet

For the first few weeks, Daniel slept. He was tired. He slept for days at a time, only waking for a drink and a sandwich before dragging himself to bed again. He barely moved. He pulled the blankets over his head. He did not hear the storms as they swept through one after the other. The wretched churn of the ocean outside his window. He needed to sleep. He had come a long way. He had a long way yet to go. When the weather turned fair, he was ready to rejoin the living.

After two months, he called the office and said that he wasn't coming back. A month later, Bearing Foods was put on the market and sold within days. It was an award-winning company with a turnover in the millions and a diverse range of low-fat snack bars that all looked like squirrel crap. Daniel's father didn't mind. Daniel certainly didn't mind. He hadn't worn socks since he arrived.

Next to go was the apartment and the car. They were nice, but they were not needed anymore. He doubted his neighbours would even notice that he was gone. He was never there anyway.

Daniel spent the time with his father. He learnt how to fish and mend lobster pots and tie up a boat and feed the chickens and dig potatoes and fix the generator. They walked together everyday. He had blisters and sunburn and sore feet, and each experience was new to him.

He still had much to learn.

seal

Daniel was floating on his back in the lee of the harbour wall. The water was cold. This was the North Atlantic, not a hotel swimming pool.

He was fully dressed again. He had a thick wetsuit on. And neoprene gloves and shoes. He could feel the ebb and swirl of the current and the rising of the tide. He was just floating. Like he had so many times before. He was looking up at the sky. Trying to gather his thoughts. He was aware that he was being watched.

He thought it might be a seal. The local grey seals were playful and curious and often came to watch him while he bobbed around in the shallows questioning his own existence. It wasn't a seal.

There was a dog watching him from the harbour wall. He hadn't seen the dog before. The nearest house was eight miles away. He wondered how the dog got there. The dog was watching him intently. Its ears were up. It barked. It was not an angry bark or a 'what are you doing?' bark. It was a 'hello' kind of bark. Then the dog disappeared.

Daniel turned over onto his front and swam for the shore.

The Map of Us

The water was so clear he could see the lazy strands of kelp beneath him and the reflection of the clouds above, and the two things seemed as one.

more cake

Daniel struggled out of his wetsuit and had a lukewarm shower. The plumbing in the former shooting lodge was a little hit and miss. There were nine bedrooms, all with ensuite bathrooms, but only five had decent water pressure. Of those five, three were in the exposed east wing and too far away from the antiquated boiler to expect anything other than a tepid drizzle once all the air locks had banged and clattered their way through the tangle of poorly lagged pipe work.

Daniel's room was on the first floor of the main building and had a bath and a shower that were both consistently lukewarm. It was better than nothing. He dried himself on a thin, scratchy towel. It had a coat of arms embroidered on it. The towels came with the lodge. They were probably forty years old. They had the absorbency of a handkerchief.

Daniel dressed quickly and made his way downstairs to the kitchen to ask his father about the dog.

'He's been hanging around since you arrived,' his father said. 'He follows you everywhere.'

'It's the first time I've seen him,' Daniel said.

'Really?' His father seemed surprised.

'Who does he belong to?' Daniel said.

'I don't think he belongs to anyone.'

'Does he have a name?'

Daniel's father shrugged.

'I'm not sure,' he said. 'But he likes cake.'

family

We were all at the house to talk about Abby. We were sitting around the kitchen table. It was a big table. It needed to be. There was me and my father and Katherine and Clive and Jack and Moss and Abby and Mr Juniper and Mrs Haddon the social worker.

Mrs Haddon and my father knew each other. Sort of. Her husband was called Donald Haddon. Until recently he had been a respected member of the sand sculpting community. Then he got caught cheating. He had secret pockets sewn into his shorts full of quick drying cement that was the same colour as the sand. He was disqualified. Four times Regional Champion. National Finalist eight years in a row. No wonder. He was stripped of all his titles. Mrs Haddon and my father sat at opposite ends of the table.

Abby sat next to Mr Juniper. It was her choice. We didn't make her sit there. She looked at his gloves.

gloves

Mr Juniper wore a pair of leather gloves. He rarely took them off. Rarer still in company. In all the time that I have known him, I have only seen his hands once.

They are burnt. They are raw and painful. They are made of red crumpled paper that looks still wet. He has no fingernails to speak of. He is now ninety-two years old and he has lived with red paper hands for the last eighty years. He does not complain.

It happened when he was young. His brother pushed him into the fireplace and kept him there. Watched. It was not an accident.

The twelve-year-old Charles Sidney Juniper liked to play the piano and was particularly fond of jazz. He played well. His brother could not. There was more to it than that.

His brother liked to keep things in jars. Live things. Whatever he could find. Whatever he could catch. Not to look at. But to shake and drown and leave in the sun and pry at with tweezers and harass with matches. He stabbed snails with pins. He caught minnows and added salt to the water a teaspoon at a time. He trapped mice in an upturned bottle. There was no telling what he did with those.

His brother did not like the sound of the piano. More particularly he did not like the sound of melodic minor scales or bebop. He could not play them. His fingers would not sit happily on the keys. He had hands designed for stabbing and prying and drowning.

His brother cornered a spider protecting its eggs and burnt it with a candle. Then he followed the sound of jazz in search of larger prey.

Mr. Juniper knew the price of cruelty. He had paid it.

resilient

Mrs Haddon had gone. Abby would be staying with Katherine and Clive indefinitely. She had no other family. Not that could be found. We were her closest relatives. There were still some formalities to deal with. Mrs Haddon would come back. She did not know when. Abby's welfare was all that mattered.

Abby sat at the big table in the kitchen surrounded by people she didn't know. She ate toast and had a drink and drew a dragon on a piece of paper with a green pen while everyone talked about her. When it was finished, she gave the picture to my father. Then she changed pens and started another picture. She was drawing Mr Juniper. First she drew his gloves. Then his moustache. She was a strange, resilient, clever child. She had to be. But she was not alone anymore. Abby had us now.

We seemed like a nice bunch. That's what Mrs Haddon said as she left. Mr Juniper didn't hum too much. Jack didn't mention the colour blue. Katherine didn't talk about hand-bags. Clive didn't mention gum disease or root canal work. I didn't say anything about low-fat snack bars or 10.37am.

My father didn't mention sand. It was for the best. We were very well behaved. We were a family. We were strange and resilient, too.

always

I found Abby standing in the doorway of Violet's study. She was staring at the painted walls as two generations of the North family had done before her.

I watched as she explored the map of Arthur Galbraith's Great Moor. Violet's act of wild invention. Bishop's Top, then northwest to New Mountsley Yard on the ceiling. Peddlar's Oven to Nine Ways End by the window. Hallberry Bridge across to Tin Gate Mire above the fire. The gap yet to be filled by the bookcase. Only the rough outline of a river and a fording place and a ring of standing stones awaiting a name and a history.

Abby turned to me.

'It's beautiful,' she said.

'Yes,' I said.

'Can I come back?'

'Always,' I said. 'This is where you belong.'

5 things that changed

I decided to resign from Compass Applied Analytics. I needed a change. I came in early and packed all my things into a small cardboard box and pushed my chair under the desk and took my collection of coffee cups to the kitchenette and left them in the dishwasher. It took five minutes. It was still early when I got home.

Helen didn't move into my office. She was working three days a week and spending more time with her third husband who just happened to be the same person as her first husband. Their new marriage had already lasted considerably longer than the first one did. 437.5% longer. She called me to let me know. It was funny. It's a statistics thing.

Helen told me that Trish was going through a patched jeans and sneakers phase. She looked twenty years younger. The wasp had not returned.

Since leaving work, I've been staying in the house in my old room. I see a lot of my father and Abby and Mr Juniper.

Bailey Southerton often brings his children to play in the garden. One is a little older than Abby. The other is a little younger. Abby likes Mr Juniper best. They talk for hours. I don't know what they talk about. I can hear them laughing from my room.

Katherine and Clive are having their house completely redecorated. Jack said he would help, and they said no. We all laughed.

Jack and Moss have moved into my flat. It's bigger. Jack was a little concerned at first. 'Where's the couch?' he said. I said the pink sofa had gone, and Moss said 'good.' I'm sure they'll work something out.

I think about 10.37 am often. It promised so much that I didn't see at the time. There was no point filling out a Compatibility Index. I had little to go on. The result of that morning was confused and incomplete.

Bearing Foods had been sold. I had no way of contacting Daniel. I would probably never see him again.

tie

Grace liked the tie. Matt didn't like the tie. He was wearing the tie.

'I'm only helping people fill in a questionnaire,' Matt said. 'I don't see why I have to wear a tie.'

'No,' Grace corrected. 'You represent the Matilda Eastleigh Compatibility Index. You're a highly trained, impartial observer overseeing a sophisticated one-to-one relationship evaluation process.'

'Uh-huh,' Matt said.

Grace liked the tie. Matt didn't like the tie. He was wearing the tie.

'I don't need to wear a tie to lend someone a pen and show them how to tick a box,' Matt said. 'It's only a rehearsal.'

'Clients are going to pay a great deal of money for your expert analysis and advice. Wearing a tie makes you look professional and trustworthy and hides the fact that you're wearing a hideous T-shirt.'

'I like this T-shirt,' Matt said.

'Uh-huh,' Grace said.

Grace liked the tie. Matt didn't like the tie. He was wearing the tie.

'What about a different tie?' Grace said, huffing a little.

'How different?' Matt said hopefully.

'Not so different that you aren't wearing one,' Grace said.

'Oh,' Matt said.

'Right,' Grace said.

'Uh-huh,' Matt said.

'Yes,' Grace said.

'Great,' Matt said.

Grace liked the tie. Matt didn't like the tie. He was wearing the tie.

the Matilda Eastleigh Compatibility Index

Section 5: Conflict Resolution

Q.47. *How often did you argue?*
(Please tick one)
Regularly
Occasionally
Rarely
Never

'We never argued. We got even.'

'Okay,' Matt said. He was wearing the tie.

'Once he hid my celebrity gossip magazine behind a cushion.'

'Right,' Matt said.

'So I retaliated by getting an extra hole put in all his belts to make him think he was putting on weight. I had it done professionally at the cobblers and dry cleaners in the high street. You really couldn't tell. He certainly didn't. He changed his diet and cut out coffee and dairy products and reduced his cholesterol level and joined the gym and went running every other day and lost nearly a stone in the first month and met someone else and left me.'

'Oh,' Matt said.

'I think we should have argued more.'

Grace liked the tie. Matt didn't like the tie. He was wearing the tie.

'Uh-huh,' Matt said.

maybe ten

Regional finals.
No one here.
Just me and a kid with a bucket.
Yellow.
Pink handle.
Plastic spade.
Knows what he's doing.
Seen him before.
Nine.
Maybe ten.
Lives on the beach.
Row of houses by the car park.
Lives in the one on the end.
Chain link fence around a garden of sand.
Private sand.
Sign says so.
Sand belongs to the houses.
Beach is about a mile.
Dunes then a golf course.
Kid knows his sand.

The Map of Us

No shoes on.
Hood up.
Over his eyes.
Tricky customer.
Raining harder now.
Coming in off the sea.
Just getting started.
Me and him.
Beach is empty.
Dog walker.
Another dog walker.
Amusement arcade is closed.
Cafe is closed.
Toilets are closed.
Should've been postponed.
Cancelled.
Said so.
Told the judge.
In his car.
In the car park.
Staying dry.
Said so.
Told him.
Regional finals.
No one here.
Just me and a kid with a bucket.
Kid who knows his sand.
Lives here.
Home advantage.

Didn't want to know.
German car.
Two-door.
Says it all.
Tide's out.
Four hours to go.
Haven't even started.
Big and bold.
No point getting out the brushes.
Palette knives.
Spatulas.
Melon baller.
Nothing clever.
Nothing the rain can wash away.
Not a swan.
Not the day for a swan.
A turtle maybe.
Just him and me.
Can't see what he's making.
Can't see.
Still trenching sand.
Building a core.
I'm going with a turtle.
Kid knows his sand.
Knows how it moves.
Works with his hands.
His feet.
Pushing.
Scooping.

The Map of Us

Shaping.
In constant motion.
Hood over his eyes.
Yellow bucket.
Plastic spade.
Can't see what it is.
Can't see what he's making.
Now I can.
I can see the outline forming.
I can just make it out.
It's a dolphin.
Bollocks.

merit

David North was building a new case against his sister. Not Violet exactly, but her daughter Rose. It was an angle of attack that David thought had some merit. He had evidence. He could make it sound compelling enough. He made a list.

First. Violet was married to a man with only one name. That was a start. A good start. It meant nothing in law, but it showed a clear failure of good sense on her part.

Second. She had chosen to conceive a child, ignoring the advice given to her by her doctors. She had willfully continued with the pregnancy despite any number of warnings that it would endanger her health and the health of her unborn child. David was sure he could find expert witnesses that were prepared to testify. For a small fee.

Third. Violet lived in a house with a large garden. The garden was no doubt full of hidden dangers for a small child. Poisonous plants perhaps. Foxes. David could not remember if the garden had a pond or not. A certain risk of drowning would be helpful. He would have to return one night and investigate by torchlight.

Fourth. Violet was clearly deluded and unstable. She lived

in an imaginary world and wrote as a man and was unable to distinguish between reality and invention. David had several volumes of *Galbraith's Boot* to support his argument. He knew he would have to go to some lengths to keep the case out of the newspapers for fear of harming sales.

Fifth and finally and most damning of all. Violet was physically unable to deal with a young child due to her long-standing infirmity and other complications. David did not know what these complications might be, but he had recently stolen a medical dictionary from the library and was making notes of ailments with the most outlandish names. It did not matter if these were false. They would make an impression, and Violet would have to refute them.

David felt confident that he could prove that Violet was an unfit mother. That the child should be taken from her and placed in the care and control of her close family. There was no malicious intent. None at all. It was for her own good and the good of the child.

He could make it all go away – for a price.

Yes. It was a route that had merit. He was sure of it.

dark road

When Mr Charles S. Juniper was informed that David North was planning on bringing new proceedings against Violet, he knew exactly what he must do.

He had hoped that it would never come to this, but David North would not be stopped by any other means. He could see that now. David knew only one road, and he would not deviate from it until he was satisfied he had reached his destination. The place he thought he deserved. He would never be happy there and would always want to travel a mile or two further. And then a mile or two more. He had to be dissuaded. His road dismantled. Thoroughly.

Mr Juniper knew in his heart that he was not the man to do the work – but he knew someone who was. Perhaps it would not go that far. Perhaps un-corking the bottle would not be needed. Perhaps shaking it would be enough. Perhaps the tragic theatre of the moment would be all that was required. It was not unlawful. Not all of it. Parts of it were. Small parts. He slipped a set of lock picks into his coat pocket. There were now few doors in London that were sufficient to keep him out.

Then Mr Juniper got in his car and went to visit his brother. Another dark road that was not to his liking. But it had to be done.

nice

David North was making his way back to the hotel room that he could not afford. He always stayed in nice hotels that he could not afford. Not luxurious, but nice. There were only really five or six truly luxurious hotels in London. He had not stayed in any of them. Nor would he. Two weeks and the game would be up. Nice hotels were nice enough. He didn't need gold-plated bath handles and monogrammed towels and a butler service night and day. Nice hotels would do. Clean baths with taps that worked. Soft white towels on a heated brass rail. Handwritten menus and room service just an internal phone call away. Staff that called you 'sir' and didn't look you directly in the eyes. There was a rich seam of such places in London. He could take his pick.

David had just dined in a fine restaurant that was beyond his means. The food was rich and swimming in oil, and all the plates were cold. He did not feel bad paying for the meal with a signed cheque from a well-known and highly exclusive private bank. It was not his bank. The cheque was stolen. He had two left. Perhaps tomorrow he would journey to the Strand and see who walked by with gaping pockets.

He arrived at his nice hotel, and there was no one available to open the door for him. It was disappointing, but it was to be expected. He made his way through the lobby, past the night porter sitting behind the reception desk reading a newspaper. He looked up, but David ignored him. He went back to reading his paper. That was good. David did not like to be recognised or remembered. He would be vacating his room shortly without paying the bill.

David made his way up to his room. The lift was out of order. A common problem with hotels that were nice. He had to take the stairs. They were not marble. They were nice enough though. For hotel stairs.

He smiled to himself. Nice hotels had pretensions. His room number would suggest that it was on the tenth floor, but it was not. It was on the first. There were glass-paneled double doors at the top of the stairs. David pushed his way through, turned right, and made his way along the corridor.

The fire exits were clearly marked and securely chained and padlocked. That was a good sign. Nice hotels always took the comfort and security of their guests seriously.

The carpet in the corridor was satisfactory. Not as nice as the hotel he had stayed in previously. It was deep and red and silent, and he could still see the tyre tracks left by the chambermaid's heavily laden linen trolley.

He had reached Room 1037. He was home. David unlocked the door and went inside. Two men were waiting for him.

imagine

Mr Charles S. Juniper was sitting on the edge of the bed. Another man was sitting with him. He had a wiry beard and appeared to be drunk.

'Do you play the piano, Mr North?' Mr Juniper said.

'No,' David replied. 'What are you doing in my room?'

'What a pity,' Mr Juniper said. 'They have a respectable baby grand in the bar downstairs. I would so love to hear it played. The room is large and the ceiling high. The acoustics should be delightful.'

'You didn't answer my question,' David said.

'Indeed not,' Mr Juniper said. 'I have had the acquaintance of many scurrilous fellows in my time. Let us just say that your door was not adequately locked and leave it at that.'

David heard the sprung door close behind him. 'What do you want?'

'Merely the opportunity to introduce you to my brother,' Mr Juniper said.

David assumed he meant the man sitting next to him on the bed. There was no one else in the room.

'Perhaps some other time,' he stuttered.

'Why wait? We are all together now,' said Mr Juniper.

The bearded man started clawing at the bedclothes with his fingers.

'What is wrong with him?' David said.

'Straight to the point then? Very well. For many years he has been chained, electrocuted and drugged,' Mr Juniper said. 'Sadly, my brother does not hear voices. They hear him. Am I making myself clear, Mr North?'

'Not really. I would like you both to leave now.'

'Why, of course,' Mr Juniper said. 'In a moment. First there is something I would like you to see.'

Mr Juniper took off his leather gloves. Slowly and deliberately. Then turned his hands over in the light of the bedside lamp.

David North could feel the sweat pool in his shoes.

'If my brother could do this to me, Mr North, imagine what he might do to you if I asked.'

jazz

The case against Violet was never brought to court. Papers went missing. Witnesses were quietly paid off. David North vanished. Owners of nice hotels and fine restaurants throughout the city would have rejoiced had they known.

Mr Juniper never mentioned his involvement in the matter. Not to anyone. He was not proud of what he had done, but it served a purpose, and it was a task that was undertaken with the best intentions.

His brother had been returned to the locked room with padded canvas wallpaper. He was happy there, torturing imaginary bugs in imaginary glass jars. If he had enjoyed his trip to London he never spoke of it. The jazz in his mind was too loud.

Sometimes justice and the law were not the best of bedfellows. The law was caught in a straight-jacket of words and precedents and adjournments and lawyer's fees and tradition and indifference. This way was better. This way was swift and clean. This way meant that Violet would not be made to stand alone in a courtroom by a man who paid for his supper with stolen cheques and had the moral compass of a jackdaw. This way meant that he would never attempt the same thing again.

David North had vanished. He was pursued by a lending library for the theft of a book from the reference section. They could not find him. No one could.

waiting

'Walks from Quarry Pound to Cleavey Down Falls' was the last book that Violet completed before she died.

It was a shorter volume than the others. It contained more sketches. She knew her life was coming to end. Time was short.

She typed slowly. She made many mistakes. She had thought of that. She had scissors and a stapler at the ready. She would cut out those passages with the fewest errors and staple them to a clean piece of paper. Often a line at a time. Sometimes a single word. 130 pages took her six months.

Violet wrapped the finished manuscript in brown paper and sent it to Ruth Pennywheal to be proofread and corrected where necessary. There was nothing more to be done. The Great Moor was beginning to fade.

She kissed each of her grandchildren on the head. She told her daughter not to cry. Then she went to bed and did not come down for breakfast. She was elsewhere. Looking for a man with one name and a wheelbarrow who said that he would love her forever. She would not need to travel far. He was waiting for her.

After her death, a cloth was put over the turquoise blue Royal Quiet Deluxe typewriter and the door to the study was closed.

Arthur Galbraith could not be consoled.

tap water

Daniel sat on the beach with his toes buried in the pure white sand. The dog sat next to him. He followed him everywhere. Daniel didn't know why he hadn't noticed the dog before. There were lots of things he was noticing for the first time.

The dog wandered off to chase a clump of dry seaweed that was slowly cartwheeling down the beach on the evening breeze. He liked cake and biscuits and sandwiches. He wasn't fussy which.

Daniel didn't know where the dog had come from. He didn't have a collar. No one had turned up looking for him. He didn't have a name other than 'Dog.' That seemed to suffice.

He did not belong to Daniel. That much was certain. They were fellow travelers. Friends.

Daniel didn't have many friends. He never had time for them. He worked too hard to keep in touch. To remember birthdays or anniversaries. He forgot. He let people down. Some things were not so easy to forget.

Daniel remembered two glasses of tap water and a spoon fight over chocolate ice cream and cheating to pay the bill and the girl in the swimming pool who saw him at his most helpless and still took him in her arms.

He knew he had to go back. He had to try.

extra

Daniel got a call from the hire company at Stornoway airport wondering when he was going to return their car. It was time enough.

Daniel said goodbye to his father. He packed some jeans and some T-shirts and borrowed a few thin, scratchy towels. There were hundreds stacked in a cupboard by the boiler. They were probably forty years old. He didn't think they would be missed.

Daniel put some shoes and socks on. It felt strange. He got back in the car and drove a little east and then north and paid the fine and the extra hire charges and flew back to London via Inverness. He had unfinished business to attend to.

He took the dog with him.

next?

I didn't know what to do next. I had a fairly good degree in Economics and Data Sciences. I could probably have worked a little harder and got a better degree. Maybe if I had worked a little harder and got a better degree I wouldn't have ended up compiling sophisticated market research on low-fat snack bars. I could have done something more interesting and rewarding instead. I don't know what. But I had a pretty good time not working any harder. I try not to think of low-fat snack bars as some kind of punishment. It isn't always easy.

I don't eat low-fat snack bars very often. We used to get lots of free samples in the office. I prefer chocolate. Maybe if I had worked a little harder and got a better degree I could be compiling sophisticated market research on chocolate instead. Yeah. Maybe I should have worked a little harder and stayed in and studied.

Damn.

lawnmower

I had nothing else to do — so I broke the lawnmower. I didn't mean to. The grass was too long. The lawnmower couldn't cope. It kept getting clogged up. Now it was stuck. The grass was knee deep in some places. Deeper in others. It needed cutting. I thought I'd do it. No one else would. It seemed like a good idea. It wasn't.

Now the lawnmower was broken. It was not the only one. There were others. There was a lawnmower stuck in the grass by the sandpit. And another stranded in the really long grass by the fence. I couldn't see it, but I knew it was there. The grass had grown over it. It's been stuck there for some time. Years. I didn't break that one. That was someone else. Jack. Or my father. We don't really look after our lawnmowers. The lawn must think we're idiots. It's not really a lawn anymore. It was once. Now it isn't.

I only managed to cut a small rectangle of grass before I broke the lawnmower. Then I gave up cutting the lawn and made Mr Juniper a pot of tea instead.

Technically the lawnmower wasn't really broken. Just stuck. Incapable of going any further.

I knew the feeling.

opening

A wasp came to the garden. Over the walls topped with cement and tall shards of broken glass. They were no barrier to a wasp of audacity and cunning.

It was looking for a new home. It had recently been evicted. The wasp was angry and out of sorts. It found an apple tree. There were damp grass cuttings beneath and an abandoned lawn mower and a job barely started.

There was a bench and an old man snoring and a pot of tea. Perhaps sometimes there was jam? Or marmalade?

The wasp felt better. This was the place.

The wasp looked for a hole in the tree. An opening. It soon found one. It went inside.

The wasp was not welcome.

The garden waited.

There was still time.

fault

There were no peaches again this year. Or pears. The honey-suckle and wisteria and clematis and ivy had spread across the south-facing wall again. As they had done before. It was their nature to do so. What did they care for peaches or pears? There was no one in the house who would dissuade them.

The wrought iron fence needed painting. There were slates missing from the potting shed roof. Brambles and stinging nettles were encroaching on the gravel paths. The circular lawns were gone. The glasshouse was full of last year's tomato plants. Withered and turned grey. No one had thought to clear it.

The garden was patient. As all gardens are. As they have to be. It was not the garden's fault.

The North family were many things.

They were not gardeners.

errands

Wednesday was a day of errands. Some more important than others.

First I called at the offices of Twelvetrees, Juniper and Brompton on the third floor of 14a Sneed Street, London. The car behaved. The traffic was kind. I found a place to park outside. It was a good start.

I went to sign a contract. A simple agreement that allowed Matt and Grace to use my Compatibility Index for relationship counselling in return for a small percentage of the profits.

It seemed important. It wasn't. Not really.

Celia Brompton drew up the papers. She was daughter of one of the original partners. I've known her since I was a child. Their offices are full of Violet's sketches. All hills and valleys and clouds and rivers. They are on every wall. It always makes me smile.

I looked through the contract. There were half a dozen pages of dense type. I didn't understand a word. I signed. Celia said to send her love to Mr Juniper. I said I would.

Next I had to go and collect six bags of premium quality washed play sand for my father's practice sandpit in the garden.

The National Sand Sculpture Finals were only a few days away. His chosen subject was proving tricky.

It seemed important. It wasn't.

My father always liked to have at least half a ton of fresh sand in reserve. Just in case of emergencies. He kept the bags in the garage. Usually leaning up against a broken washing machine. I said I'd collect the sand as long as he bought more ice cream. We had a deal.

Then I had to swing past a speciality fish importer for Jack.

It seemed important. It wasn't.

Jack wanted to get hold of farmed freshwater Marron crayfish from Western Australia. He had a recipe he wanted to try out. It was a surprise for Moss. Marron came in a variety of different colours. Red, brown, black- even striped. A rare variant were bright blue. Those were the ones that Jack wanted.

They didn't have any.

I stopped for a coffee and a warm buttery croissant.

I made another stop nearby to deliver some glass shelves that Katherine had promised to a friend who was opening a new and exclusive pre-loved handbag shop.

It seemed important. It wasn't.

Apparently the shelves were too long or too short or not what she was expecting. I couldn't make out what she was saying. She clucked a lot. I was illegally parked and running late. I said if she didn't want the shelves I'd leave them in the car, and then she clucked a bit more and said she'd take them as if she was doing me a huge favour. I had to carry them into the shop myself.

Finally I went to pick up Ruth Pennywheal. She was coming to stay with us for a few days. When I turned into her road I could see she was already waiting outside. She had a small brown suitcase with her. She gave me a lengthy and robust hug and climbed carefully into the passenger seat. I could tell she was nervous.

'Does Sidney know I'm coming?' she said.

'Yes,' I said.

'What did he say?'

I turned to Ruth and took her hand. It was cold.

'He hasn't stopped singing,' I said.

I indicated to pull out, found first gear – on the third attempt – and headed in the direction of home.

Ruth Pennywheal was coming to stay.

Mr Juniper would be happy.

That was important.

undone

Mr Juniper could not say her name.

He wanted to. He tried. The words would not come. He clicked and hummed. He had tears in his eyes. They were not tears of sadness or frustration. They were tears that said everything that he had wanted to say in a letter. So many years ago. All the things his hands would not allow. He had proposed, and she said no. It was a mistake.

He could not say her name.

He did not have to.

Ruth was with him now.

They sat together under the apple tree. On the wrought iron bench that Owen had found in the garden. And Mr Juniper sang to her.

'Isn't it wonderful,' my father said.

We were standing by the back door. I didn't say anything.

My father had a special 'wonderful' that was reserved for Sidney alone. It had a great deal of joy in it. It was subtle and hard to explain. It had grown. Now it was big enough for two.

I gave my father a lengthy and robust hug. It seemed appropriate somehow. Then we went inside.

It seemed that some mistakes could be undone.

wanted

There was a notice board in the village. Outside the church. It was made by someone with only rudimentary carpentry skills. It had clearly been repaired many times since by others who possessed only a primitive understanding of the size of nail or screw that was appropriate. The wood was cracked and splintered. There were metal plates at the corners, glued wedges and a little string. The glass door swung perfectly on its hinges.

I pinned up the notice. I wrote it by hand.

It was the right thing to do. We all agreed it was for the best. We could not go on as we were. We needed help.

The notice was short and colourful.

'Gardener Required.'

I used a purple pencil and then drew daisies around the words in green and yellow. Then I drew a smiling bee that looked more like a wasp and decided to stop before I messed the whole thing up and had to start again.

I couldn't believe it had come to this.

the Matilda Eastleigh Compatibility Index

Section 8: Commitment & Compromise

Q.74. *How often did you say 'I love you'?*
(please tick one)
All the time
Occasionally
Rarely
Never

Grace's client couldn't decide. She hovered over the options with her pen.

'I don't know which one to tick,' she said.

'You need to be as honest as you can,' Grace said. 'The questionnaire only works if you're completely honest.'

'Yes,' her client said. 'I'm thinking.'

'Good,' Grace said. 'The next question is easier.'

'Oh. Okay. Thanks. This is harder than I thought.'

'You're doing great,' Grace said, trying to sound encouraging.

'At first it was all the time,' her client said.

'That's fine,' Grace said.

'Then it was just occasionally.'

'Okay.'

'Then it was rarely.'

'Uh-huh.'

'Then for a while it was never.'

'Right.'

'Then is was occasionally again.'

'Yes.'

'Followed by maybe a whole six months of all the time.'

'Great.'

'Then some more never.'

'Oh.'

'Then it was just assumed.'

'I think I understand'

'It didn't need to be said.'

'No.'

'It was obvious.'

'Yes.'

'Then there was a long period when it wasn't said or implied or demonstrated.'

'Oh.'

'Yeah. That was bad.'

'Sorry.'

'Then it was said again, but I didn't believe it.'

'Okay.'

'It sounded forced and cynical.'

'Uh-huh.'

'Like it was just what we both wanted to hear.'

'Yeah.'

'Going through the motions of saying it without really meaning it.'

'Right.'

'Then we got over that by not saying *it* exactly but something different that implied the same thing but in an entirely different way.'

'Great.'

'Then we stopped saying that, too.'

'Oh.'

'Or the other thing that we didn't say anymore because it sounded so fake.'

'Right.'

'Now we barely speak at all.'

'Okay.'

'Shall I skip the question?'

'Yeah.'

Grace was exhausted. She was glad she didn't need Matt to fill in a form. She already had a detailed Marriage Report with footnotes and a summary and a series of conclusions. It contained three Venn diagrams, a histogram, five pie charts, a line graph and a colour-coded flow chart. She knew the signs to look for.

So far, 'Sexual Activity' was exceeding expectations.

If things started to dwindle, Grace was going to buy some coloured pencils and a ruler. That should keep him guessing.

folly

I didn't understand. My Compatibility Index was a huge success. Matt and Grace had more bookings than they could deal with. They were thinking of hiring a second team of observers. Matt was wearing a tie, and I was more confused than ever. It didn't make any sense. None of it.

My grandmother could not walk far. My grandfather had only one name. She wrote imaginary walking guides. He was a gardener. They had next to nothing in common, and yet they were married for life. He loved her until his last breath. What they shared could not be measured or quantified or distilled into numbers or turned into a graph. I could see that now. I was foolish to have tried.

It was plain I was lost. But how lost?

My grandmother taught me that anything is possible.

My mother taught me that true happiness is a series of infinitely small things that are all too easily taken for granted.

My father taught me that nothing stays the same forever. That the world we make for ourselves is constantly changing, and that it is a better place because of it.

And I had taught myself to ignore their lessons and hide myself in numbers and the folly of certainty.

That was how lost.

ice cream

I was in the kitchen eating ice cream. There wasn't much left. I've been eating a lot of ice cream recently. Even using a small spoon, it doesn't last long.

It was chocolate ice cream. Abby's favourite was strawberry. So was Mr Juniper's. Ruth Pennywheal hadn't decided yet. She was still getting used to us. She had lived alone for years. She didn't buy ice cream. Not even for special occasions. She lived alone. There wasn't much she cared to celebrate. Now she was staying with us. A decision on her favourite ice cream was pending. If I didn't eat it all first.

My father came into the kitchen. He saw what I was eating. I thought I knew what he was going to say. Something about eating too much ice cream.

He handed me a letter instead.

'Your mum asked me to give you this when you were lost,' he said.

Dear Matilda

Just a quick note to say that I have left the remaining chapters of Volume 17: 'Rook's Wood to Coldbank Ruins' in the desk drawer. I hope you can find a moment to type them up for me. Sorry. I ran out of time.

Before you start, there are a few things you should know. The typewriter needs a new ribbon. They are hard to come by, but not impossible. You might ask Mr Southerton (Snr). He was always an expert at finding obscure parts for broken washing machines. Maybe he can do the same for typewriters, too.

Unfortunately the 'e' sticks as badly as ever. It is a simple thing to fix, but I believe that the 'a' and the 'g' are now going the same way. Press the small button on the top and it will open automatically. Unstick whichever letter is causing you trouble and replace the top. Then press the backspace key. It's an annoying process, but you soon get used to it.

Your grandmother's sketches are on the bookshelf wrapped in brown paper. They are unlabeled and all look much the same. She would choose a selection from the bottom of the pile and randomly incorporate them into the text. It is the way she taught me, and I hope you will carry on the tradition.

Once Volume 17 is complete, please give it to Ruth Pennywheal for proofreading and correction as always. If I could ask a small favour when you do. Deliver the book in person. I think Ruth is quite lonely.

If the 'e' and the 'a' and the 'g' have made you vow to go no further, then cover the typewriter again and go about your life as before. If not, perhaps you would consider writing Volume 18? There are rivers to be named and a blank wall still to be filled. The Great Moor is yours. I'm sure your grandmother would approve.

One last thing. Be patient. Arthur Galbraith is a journey. Do not expect to know him all at once.

Love
Mum x

couldn't

I was excited and apprehensive and humbled and over-whelmed. I wanted to get started right away – but I couldn't. I had gardeners to deal with.

A man turned up in a truck with a mini digger on a trailer. He said he favoured a 'bare earth' approach to gardening. He liked to flatten and eradicate everything first and then start again. He had a chainsaw and a stump grinder and gallons of weed killer and said it would probably be cheaper to pave the whole lot. I took his card and said I'd call.

I didn't call.

I wanted to reread all 16 volumes of *Galbraith's Boot*, but I couldn't – I was interrupted.

Another man turned up with an electric grass trimmer and a pair of pruning shears in a leather pouch on his belt. He looked at the garden. It was larger than he had imagined. He asked if we had an extension cable. I said we did. It wouldn't reach far. He asked if we had any odd jobs that needed doing. I said yes – gardening. He gave me his card. Reluctantly. I said I'd call.

I didn't call.

I wanted to go on long walks and get my shoes muddy and wear a wooly hat – even if I didn't need to – but I couldn't. There was always someone else getting in the way.

Then a woman turned up. She was wearing dungarees and army surplus boots and had her hair tied up in a messy bun with a hazel twig pushed through it. She said her name was 'Moonbeam Rainbow,' but it was really Fiona. She lives in the village.

She brought a rolled beeswax candle with her. She lit the candle in the garden and closed her eyes. She moved clumsily through the tall grass and brambles, wafting the candle around in increasingly erratic circles. Then she got stuck in the hedge and opened her eyes again. She said something about a deeply fulfilling spiritual connection, but I wasn't really listening. I was trying not to laugh. Then she said she was very busy and wouldn't be available until after the equinox and could we pay in advance as she had an electricity bill to pay.

She didn't leave a card. She gave me a painted pebble. It had a dandelion on it. Her number was painted on the other side. I said I'd call.

I didn't call her back either.

Several people turned up just to look around the garden. I tried to be welcoming and polite. I wasn't always successful.

sketches

National Finals.
Wasn't going to enter.
What's the point?
Tilly's fault.
Blame her.
Told me I had to.
Bailey Southerton didn't help.
Fixed the car.
Engine coolant.
Bottle of screenwash.
New headlight bulb.
No excuses.
Long drive.
Didn't overheat.
Slept in the back.
Up at dawn.
Breakfast.
More toast.
Registration.

Found my pitch.
Kid was there again.
Yellow bucket.
Pink handle.
Plastic spade.
Didn't stand a chance.
Kid knows his sand.
Lives on the beach.
Five dolphins
and a whale
and a robot octopus
and me.
Came first.
Can't believe it.
Beat them all.
Sketches.
Never tried that before.
Too complicated without.
Jack drew them.
Asked him to.
View from three sides.
Got them laminated.
Found three stones.
Put them on top.
Not going anywhere.
Tight on time.
Fifty keys and a space bar
and a ribbon

and a platen.
New dental tools from Clive.
New brushes from Jack.
New purpose from Abby.
Kid with the bucket shook my hand after.
Knows his sand.
Car started first time.
Drove home.
Long drive.
Seemed shorter.
Didn't overheat.
Tools in the kitchen sink.
Put the trophy in her room
on her desk
by the turquoise blue Royal Quiet Deluxe typewriter
that I carved in sand.
'Love you,' I said.
Then I closed the study door behind me.
Went into the garden.
Everyone was waiting.
Tilly.
Jack and Moss.
Katherine and Clive.
Abby.
Ruth Pennywheal and Mr Juniper.

And?
they said.

Jules Preston

And?

I raised my arms in the air
and everyone cheered.

wheelbarrow

It was late afternoon. Sometime in June. There was a wheel-barrow in the middle of the road.

Not quite the middle, but near enough to fit the description. There was no telling how long it had been there. It was an old wheelbarrow. It had wooden handles and a metal tub and a rimless iron wheel with spokes. It was in the middle of the road. It didn't belong in the middle of the road.

It was a quiet road. But just because it was quiet didn't make the sight of a wheelbarrow any more incongruous. Or magical.

There was no way of knowing how it got there. There was nothing in the wheelbarrow. There wasn't a note that said *'This is my wheelbarrow. Sorry it is in the middle of the road. I had to rush off and do something else and left it here. It isn't the wheelbarrow's fault. It's my fault. Please don't shout at the wheelbarrow. It is a good wheelbarrow. Sorry again. Thanks.'* There was no note of any kind. The wheelbarrow was empty.

It was the colour of rust but not rusty. It was old. It was the colour of its age and its occupation. It was a wheelbarrow left in the middle of the road. It was doing its best under difficult circumstances.

It was found by a man who had no immediate use for a wheelbarrow. He pushed the wheelbarrow to the side of the road. It was safer there. The man pushed the wheelbarrow to the side of the road and then doubted that it was any safer at the side of the road than it was in the middle. Someone might steal it. It was an old wheelbarrow. It didn't deserve to be stolen. Bad enough that someone had left in the middle of the road. It might end up in the back of a van with other stolen wheelbarrows. The man had no real grasp of the current level of wheelbarrow-related crime. He was new to the area. Being stolen would not be its fate. He decided to look after the wheelbarrow until its true owner could be found. The man pushed the wheelbarrow down the road in the direction that he was traveling. The iron wheel was well greased. The wooden handles were worn to a shine.

The man was not alone. He had a dog with him. The dog jumped into the wheelbarrow. Why walk when you can be pushed in a wheelbarrow?

The dog had lofty ideas.

'Rooks Wood to Coldbank Ruins'

Volume 17 of Galbraith's Boot was finished. Ruth Pennywheal was reading it aloud in the garden, making corrections in pencil as she went. Abby was sitting on her lap. Mr Juniper had his eyes closed, but he wasn't snoring.

I was washing out some paintbrushes in the kitchen. I've been practicing my mountains and rivers. There is a place on the wall that I have yet to fill. A hole in the map.

I know that I'm not ready. My clouds are ready. My valleys are competent, but my mountains and rivers still need work. Jack said he would help, and I said no.

I spend most of my day in the study now. Where my mother and grandmother sat. At a desk with a turquoise blue Royal Quiet Deluxe typewriter in front of me – and The Great Moor beyond, Arthur Galbraith close by, waiting to embark on another adventure. Merely the distance of paper apart.

The study is a place of beauty and sadness and longing and hope and regret and joy. It is painted on the walls all around me. But there is still something missing. A gap yet to be filled. It will take more than a paintbrush.

The typewriter is infuriating and temperamental, and now the 'm' sticks as well – but I have learned to love it despite its many shortcomings. It has a friendly clatter and a jovial 'ping' when it reaches the end of a line. I could never have it repaired. It would seem like a betrayal.

Mr Southerton (Snr) found a new ribbon. I bought two. I hope to make a start on Volume 18: 'Walks from Hinds Lot to Hallberry Bridge' soon. There are still a small number of Violet's original sketches left. There are some that my mother drew. They are different and the same.

There is a pen and some ink. There is plenty of paper. When my rivers are ready, it will be my turn.

3 miles

The man with the dog had walked from the railway station. It was 3 miles to the house he was looking for. It was a detached house made of hard white bricks surrounded by a large garden. It would take a little longer to get to than expected.

The station was closed in the late 1960s but had recently been reopened by a group of steam enthusiasts. They ran a limited service using a rebuilt saddle tank locomotive and some rolling stock that was on loan from a heritage museum. The man hadn't anticipated catching a steam train to his destination. He paid half fare for the dog.

The man bought a postcard at the gift shop. It was a photograph of the station in the 1950s. It looked exactly the same. Apart from the cars in the car park were different.

3 miles didn't seem that far to walk. The wheelbarrow changed things. The man didn't mind. It was a good wheelbarrow.

The dog didn't mind either. He had been on a steam train. Now he was being pushed in a wheelbarrow. His day was getting better by the moment.

The wheelbarrow was just happy to be a wheelbarrow again and not an unlikely obstruction in the middle of the road.

full circle

There was someone at the door. We were expecting Mrs
Haddon. I peered through the curtains in the front parlour.
It wasn't Mrs Haddon. There was a man standing on the
doorstep. He had a dog. And a wheelbarrow.

I opened the door. Only a little. The man ran a hand
through his hair and stood up straight. The dog sat down.
The two things happened simultaneously. I smiled. I couldn't
help myself. Then I knew who the man was.

'Daniel. What are you doing here?'

'I've come for you,' he said.

I nodded. It was a statement said with such complete
confidence that I felt obliged to acknowledge it in some way.
It made perfect sense to me.

'Yes,' I said.

'I'm sorry it's taken me so long,' he said.

I looked at the dog. The dog looked at me. His ears were
up. He had never been inside the house before. I looked at
the wheelbarrow. It was a good wheelbarrow. Old and strangely
familiar.

'Are you any good at gardening?' I said.

'I can dig potatoes and mend lobster pots,' Daniel said hopefully.

I thought about that for a moment.

'You'd better come in then,' I said.

They both came inside. The dog ran straight through to the garden. Daniel followed with the wheelbarrow.

It was happening again.

37 words, an unintentional smile and a rewarding nod.

We had come full circle.

Then I closed the door.

The world was complete again.

Acknowledgements

Thanks to Charlotte Ledger and Laura Macallen for their awesome editing, Laura Bambrey for her endless enthusiasm, and Nigel Doran for the clever equation.

A Q&A with Jules Preston

What was your inspiration for writing *The Map of Us*?

I liked the idea of someone who could look objectively at their failed relationship. Someone who would turn everything into a graph or a table. A character who wanted to know exactly how much they were to blame for their marriage coming to an end. Not trying to find excuses. Trying to get at the truth.

I wrote a short synopsis for the book, a little over a thousand words, and it all seemed to make perfect sense. It was clear and concise, and I had a strong idea where the story would go.

Then I sat down to actually write it, and the first chapter I finished introduced Violet North, and the house made of hard, white bricks. I had no idea who she was, or how she was related to anything. It happens like that sometimes. I'd set off in the wrong direction.

I set the chapter aside and tried again.

Next, I started writing the thoughts of man who spent his life on a beach, building sand castles. It was happening again. I set that aside too.

Then there was a world authority on the colour blue, and his sister who collected handbags to hide her grief, and a stone harbour in the Outer Hebrides, and an unknown adventurer, walking a vast Moor that only existed in the mind of a lonely woman. Good grief.

I'd been writing for a whole week and hadn't mentioned the main character, Tilly, at all. I decided to keep on going.

There were times when Violet was in serious danger of being edited out – but somehow I couldn't bring myself to do it.

The further the book progressed the more the relationships between all of the characters seem to develop. Then Mr Juniper appeared. He pulled it all together. I knew what I was doing after that.

It certainly wasn't the book I intended to write – but I found my way in the end.

Have you always wanted to be a writer?

Not really. I wanted to be an actor. I did that for a bit. Then I wanted to be a musician, so I did that for a bit too. Then I wrote a musical – which seemed to be the next logical step for an actor and musician. That earned me a commission from the BBC. So I became a writer. I wrote television for a while. I didn't think about writing a book for years.

Then, one afternoon, I started writing a book about fashion.

I don't know anything about fashion. The first chapter featured and old man driving a large green car. It had nothing to do with the story I had intended to write. I get that a lot.

I finished the book though, and put it in a drawer, where it will hopefully stay forever. Then I wrote *The Map of Us*.

How do you find time to write? And where do you write when you do?

I write when I can. Mostly in the morning. Sometimes late into the night. I tend to edit in the afternoon.

I have two, practically identical desks, that are made out of old pallets. They aren't very well made. I made them. But they've followed me around from house to house over the years and haven't fallen apart yet. I have a laptop and a pile of coloured paper on each. It's really a matter of where I sit down first. Only one of the computers is attached to the internet. If I really need to get something finished, I don't sit there.

What would you like readers to take away from *The Map of Us*?

It's a book about love. Lots of different kinds of love. Lost and found. I hope people enjoy spending time with the North family. I like them a lot. When I was editing the book, the best part was re entering their world – even for a short time. I also want to live in a large house in the Outer Hebrides, with a stone walled harbour, and its own island, and distant views to Skye.

Who are your favourite authors and have they influenced your writing in any way?

The poets, Brian Patten and Roger McGough, were a huge influence when I was growing up. Then I discovered '*In Watermelon Sugar*,' written in the late 1960s by American novelist, Richard Brautigan. It's impossible to say how many times I've bought that book and given it to friends to read, only for it to be passed on again to someone else. He started out as a poet too. He has a wonderfully quirky prose style, and writes in short chapters. His books are hard to find, but well worth the effort.

If you could run away to a paradise island, what or who would you take with you and why?

I have a small painting of the Cobb Gate Fish Bar at Lyme Regis, Dorset. It's an oil sketch on canvas, with a red moped parked outside, and distant views along the coast to Charmouth. The tide is in, and the water is muddy. I walked into a gallery, saw it, and bought it immediately. It didn't really matter how much it cost. Luckily it didn't cost as much as I thought it would.

It sits above my desk (the one with the laptop that is attached to the internet). I look at it all the time. On the first floor are two dark windows with barely painted in frames. They look back at me. It's mundane and incredibly magical. I'd take that.